The Strange Case of Dr Jekyll and Mr Hyde

化身博士

原著 Robert Louis Stevenson
改寫 Les Kirkham, Sandra Oddy and Maria Cleary
譯者 李璞良

U0025407

MP3

寂天雲 APP

如何下載 MP3 音檔

❶ **寂天雲 APP 聆聽**： 掃描書上 QR Code 下載「寂天雲 - 英日語學習隨身聽」APP。加入會員後，用 APP 內建掃描器再次掃描書上 QR Code，即可使用 APP 聆聽音檔。

❷ **官網下載音檔**：請上「寂天閱讀網」（www.icosmos.com.tw），註冊會員／登入後，搜尋本書，進入本書頁面，點選「MP3 下載」下載音檔，存於電腦等其他播放器聆聽使用。

About this Book

For the Student

Listen to the story and do some activities on the iCosmos Audio app.

Talk about the story.

For the Teacher

Go to our Readers Resource site for information on using readers and downloadable Resource Sheets, photocopiable Worksheets, and Tapescripts. www.helblingreaders.com

For lots of great ideas on using Graded Readers consult Reading Matters, the Teacher's Guide to using Helbling Readers.

Structures

Modal verb would	Non-defining relative clauses
I'd love to . . .	Present perfect continuous
Future continuous	Used to / would
Present perfect future	Used to / used to doing
Reported speech / verbs / questions	Second conditional
Past perfect	Expressing wishes and regrets
Defining relative clauses	

Structures from other levels are also included.

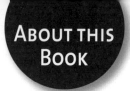

CONTENTS

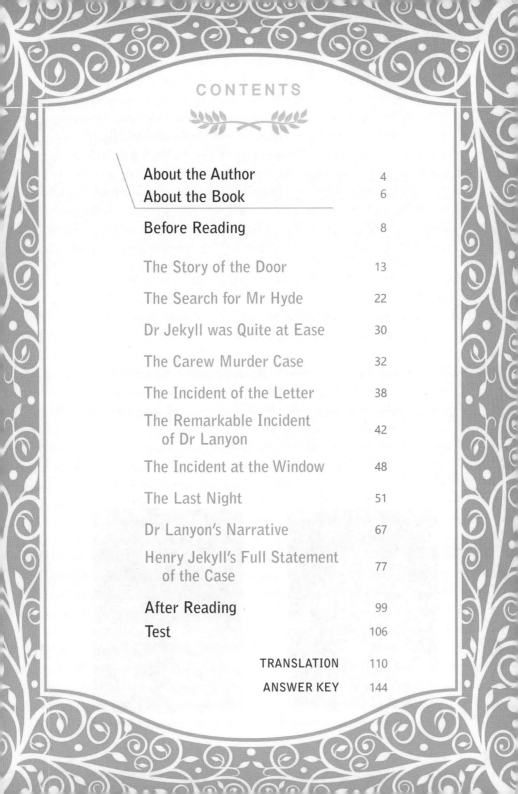

About the Author

Robert Louis Stevenson was born in Scotland in 1850. His father was a well-known engineer[1]. Robert studied engineering then law[2]. He became a full-time writer and author in 1876, and married Fanny Osbourne in 1880.

Stevenson became known for his travel writing, such as *Travels with a Donkey in the Cevennes* (1879), and adventure stories, such as *Treasure Island* (1883). He disliked the hypocrisy[3] he saw in 19th century British society and his attitudes[4] and outlook[5] are, to a 21st century reader, quite modern.

Stevenson suffered from ill health and he and Fanny traveled widely looking for a climate that would be good for him. His travels often gave him material for his writing.

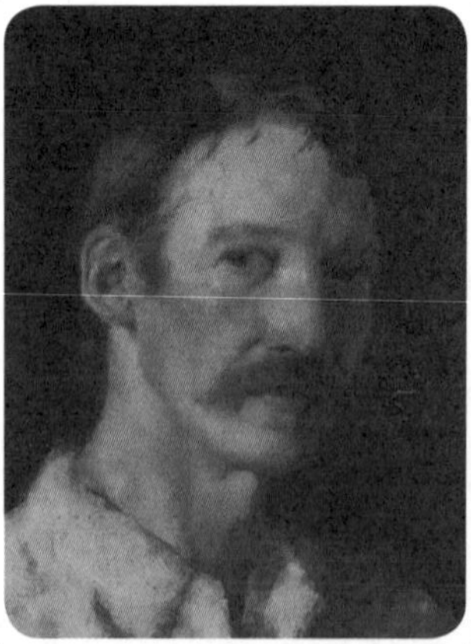

He wrote *The Strange Case of Dr Jekyll and Mr Hyde* and *Kidnapped*[6] while he and Fanny were living in Bournemouth from 1886 to 1887. This town on the south coast of England had been recommended to him for its good climate. And his father bought them a house here as a wedding present.

After 1887, his search for a more adventurous life and healthier climate led Robert and Fanny to travel around Europe, then the Pacific Ocean. In 1889 they set up house[7] on the Pacific island of Samoa, where Stevenson died in 1894.

Stevenson remains a popular author wherever English is spoken, and he is also remembered in France, where his *Travels with a Donkey in the Cevennes* has helped the revival[8] of the tourist industry[9] in that area.

1 engineer [ˌɛndʒəˋnɪr] (n.) 工程師
2 law [lɔ] (n.) 法律
3 hypocrisy [hɪˋpɑkrəsɪ] (n.) 偽善；虛偽
4 attitude [ˋætətjud] (n.) 態度
5 outlook [ˋaʊtˌlʊk] (n.) 觀點；看法
6 kidnap [ˋkɪdnæp] (v.) 綁架；劫持
7 set up house 決定住在……
8 revival [rɪˋvaɪvḷ] (n.) 振興
9 tourist industry 觀光業

About the Book

The Strange Case of Dr Jekyll and Mr Hyde is possibly Stevenson's most famous book. And the phrase "Jekyll and Hyde" (as in the expression "he is a Jekyll and Hyde character") has become a very common saying in English, and is well-known even by people who have not read the book.

The main theme of the book is the "divided self[1]" or the 'dual[2]' nature of man. It is centered around the belief that good and evil are present in all of us and explores what could happen if these parts were chemically divided into two separate personalities. It is a theme that was particularly dear[3] to Stevenson who had already developed a play and a short story on it.

The story also looks at the importance of reputation[4]. The respectable[5] Dr Jekyll starts his transformation into the evil Mr Hyde because he is afraid his behavior is inappropriate and he wants to save his reputation. His friends Utterson, Lanyon and Enfield avoid gossip[6] at all costs. The importance of reputation also reflects the importance of appearances and facades[7] in Victorian society and how, very often, the surface hides a sordid[8] and violent reality.

The story's structure is also interesting. In addition to the narrative told by the writer, we have two descriptions of the same events written by characters in the story. We read the same part of the story three times, but from three different points of view.

The story has been translated into many languages and been the inspiration for a number of films, musicals, plays, stories, cartoons and videogames.

1 divided self 分裂的自我
2 dual [ˋdjuəl] (a.) 雙重的
3 dear [dɪr] (a.) 珍視的
4 reputation [ˏrɛpjəˋteʃən] (n.) 名譽；聲望
5 respectable [rɪˋspɛktəbḷ] (a.) 值得尊敬的；名聲好的
6 gossip [ˋgɑsəp] (n.) 閒話
7 facade [fəˋsɑd] (n.) 假象
8 sordid [ˋsɔrdɪd] (a.) 骯髒的；污穢的

Before Reading

1 Look at these scenes from the book. Discuss with a partner.

(a) What is happening in each scene?
(b) What happens next in each scene?
(c) Think of a title for each picture.

2 Look at the pictures again. Write five questions about each one. Ask and answer the questions with a partner then compare your answers with the rest of the class.

3 Look through the illustrations in the story. Do you recognize any of the characters from the scenes above? How are the illustrations similar to the two scenes above? What atmosphere do the illustrations suggest? What elements of the illustrations add to the atmosphere (colors, light, style, and subject)?

4 What do you know about the story of Dr Jekyll and Mr Hyde? Brainstorm in class.

5 Listen to Dr Jekyll speaking. Then tick (✓) T (true) or F (false) below.

T F (a) Mr Hyde is more evil than Dr Jekyll.
T F (b) Dr Jekyll is taller than Mr Hyde.
T F (c) Mr Hyde is younger than Dr Jekyll.
T F (d) Dr Jekyll is uglier than Mr Hyde.
T F (e) Mr Hyde is mixture of good and evil.
T F (f) Mr Hyde has got a kindly face.

6 Look at three pictures below. Which one is Mr Hyde? Give reasons for your choice.

a

b

c

7 The story is set in Victorian London. In groups find out as much as you can about life at that time. Write a description of your daily life in Victorian London.

8 Read the chapter titles in the book. Then listen and match each title with the correct summary.

_____ (a) The Story of the Door
_____ (b) The Search for Mr Hyde
_____ (c) Dr Jekyll was Quite at Ease
_____ (d) The Carew Murder Case
_____ (e) The Incident of the Letter
_____ (f) The Remarkable Incident of Dr Lanyon
_____ (g) The Incident at the Window
_____ (h) The Last Night
_____ (i) Dr Lanyon's Narrative
_____ (j) Henry Jekyll's Full Statement of the Case

9 Here are some of the characters from the book. Read what they say. Can you guess who they are?

1 
Dr Lanyon

2 
Mr Enfield

3 
Mr Utterson

4 
Dr Jekyll

_____ (a) I'm a doctor, and I used to be a friend of Dr Jekyll's. I do not like the experiments Jekyll is working on.

_____ (b) I'm a friend of Utterson's. We often go walking together.

_____ (c) I'm a doctor, and a friend of Utterson's. I'm doing experiments into the nature of man.

_____ (d) I'm Jekyll's friend and lawyer. I've been worried about him recently.

10 Who is Mr Hyde? Read the back cover of the book and use what you know to make a guess. Discuss in groups.

11 Here are some words that appear in the story. Match them with the pictures.

______	(a) axe	______	(e) measuring glass
______	(b) doorknocker	______	(f) powder
______	(c) chimney	______	(g) walking-stick
______	(d) chain	______	(h) ashes

1

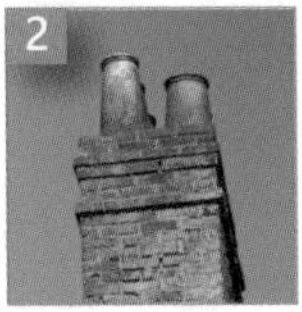
2

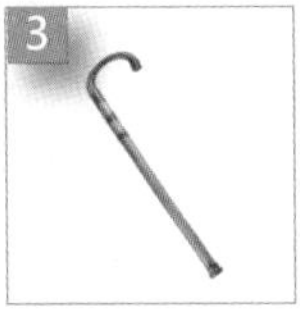
3

4

5

6

7

8

12 Use the words above to complete these sentences.

(a) He started hitting the gentleman with a thick ______________.

(b) He put some of the red liquid into the ______________.

(c) There was some salt-like ______________ wrapped in paper.

(d) They found a pile of ______________ in the cold fireplace.

(e) Poole swung the ______________ and smashed the wooden panels of the door.

(f) Someone must live there because there is usually smoke coming from the ______________.

(g) The door was opened on the ______________ by a female servant.

(h) The door was scratched and dirty and had no ______________.

The Story of the Door

Mr Utterson was a lawyer, and a man of some contradictions[1]. He hardly ever smiled, so he looked rather unfriendly and unwelcoming. But, in company with[2] friends, and at parties, he was quite social and companionable[3]. He did not allow himself many luxuries[4], and did not spend much money on himself at all. Although he enjoyed fine wines, he did not drink them when alone. He enjoyed the theater, but had not gone to see a play for twenty years. However, he was happy to see others enjoy themselves, and did not complain or criticize[5] them for allowing an excess[6] of pleasure in their lives. Because of this he was often one of the last respectable friends of men who were losing their good reputation and going downwards in society.

He could be called modest[7], for he was good-natured to his friends and did not expect them to follow his example. He accepted them as they were, faults[8] and all. His companions were usually distant relations from his own family, or friends that he had known for a long time. You could say that he did not choose his friends, but they gradually collected around him in time, like ivy[9] grows on a tree.

1 contradiction [ˌkɑntrəˋdɪkʃən] (n.) 矛盾；抵觸
2 in company with 與……在一起
3 companionable [kəmˋpænjənbḷ] (a.) 好相處的
4 luxury [ˋlʌkʃərɪ] (n.) 奢華；奢侈品
5 criticize [ˋkrɪtɪˌsaɪz] (v.) 批評；評論
6 excess [ɪkˋsɛs] (n.) 無節制；過度
7 modest [ˋmɑdɪst] (a.) 端莊的；有節制的
8 fault [fɔlt] (n.) 錯誤；過失
9 ivy [ˋaɪvɪ] (n.) 常春藤

5

One friend in particular was Mr Richard Enfield, a distant relative, and a well-known man in the city of London. The two men were very different, but they always went for a long Sunday walk together.

People who saw them out on their walk reported that they rarely spoke, often looked unhappy, and always seemed to welcome the sight of other friends. However, it is a fact that the two men looked forward to[1] these weekly walks. They would even cancel other appointments in order to go and enjoy their walks without interruption.

Friends

- Who are your closest friends? What do you like to do with them?
- Do you enjoy doing different things with different friends?

One day, while they were out on their walk together, they were strolling[2] along a small quiet street in an otherwise busy[3] area of London. It was now quiet because it was Sunday and most of the shops were closed. But during the week the shops and businesses in that street were busy, and most were successful. It was a pleasant, colorful street, which was kept clean and attractive by the people who lived and worked there. Or rather[4] it was all clean and attractive except for one building, two storeys[5] high, next to an open passage that led away from the street.

1 look forward to 期待（後接名詞或動名詞）
2 stroll [strol] (v.) 散步；溜達
3 otherwise busy 一向很忙碌
4 or rather 說得更確切些
5 storey [ˋstorɪ] (n.)〔英〕樓層
6 crumbling [ˋkrʌmbl̩ɪŋ] (a.) 碎裂的

6 This building had no windows facing the street, and its bare, unfriendly wall was broken only by a door at ground level. The wall was discolored and crumbling[6] and the door was scratched[7] and dirty, with peeling[8] paint. It had no bell or doorknocker. It looked uncared for, and the scratches and writing that had been left by children had not been cleaned or repaired.

As they passed, Mr Enfield asked Mr Utterson if he had ever noticed the door, because it reminded him of a very strange story.

"No," said Mr Utterson. "What story was that?"

"Well," replied Mr Enfield. "Once, I was coming home this way at about 3 a.m. on a dark winter's night, and the whole area was very quiet and deserted[9]. It was so quiet that I thought to myself, 'If I see a policeman I will feel safer.' But then suddenly I saw two people. One was a small unpleasant-looking man walking along this street at a good speed. The second was a small girl, about eight or nine years old, running as fast as she could along another street which led into this one. Well, the two met at the corner and ran into[10] each other. The unusual thing was that instead of stopping and apologizing[11], the little man, quite on purpose[12], stamped[13] hard on the girl as she lay on the ground, screaming with pain. Then he walked on, leaving her there.

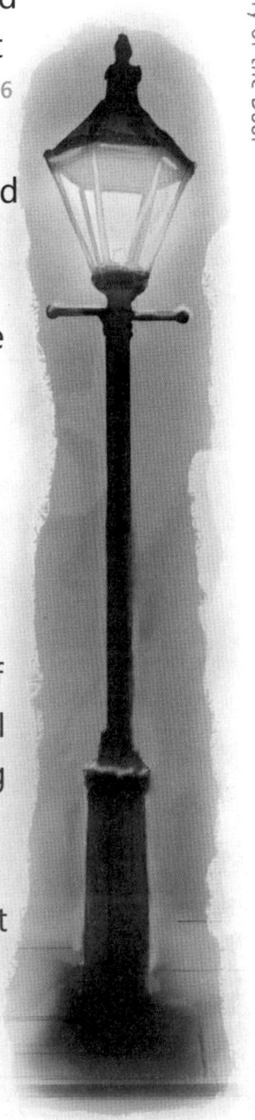

7 scratch [skrætʃ] (v.) 擦；刮；亂劃
8 peeling [ˋpilɪŋ] (a.) 削落的
9 deserted [dɪˋzɜtɪd] (a.) 廢棄的
10 run into 撞到
11 apologize [əˋpɑləˏdʒaɪz] (v.) 道歉
12 on purpose 故意
13 stamp [stæmp] (v.) 踩

"It was a terrible thing to see. It was as if the man was not human at all, more a powerful, unstoppable machine. I shouted out and chased the man, caught him and brought him back to where he had knocked down the girl.

"The noise had attracted a small crowd of people, including some of the girl's family, who were very angry with the man. A doctor arrived and examined the poor girl, who was more frightened than hurt. The man was quiet and did not try to escape[1], but the expression[2] on his face was so ugly and unpleasant that it frightened me. He did not apologize, nor was he sorry for what had happened.

"I saw that the doctor also seemed to dislike the man. We all told him that we would make a lot of trouble for him if he did not pay for his actions. And all the time we had to protect[3] him from the women who were trying to attack[4] him.

"Because there were so many angry people gathered, and because we did not stop our demands[5], the man agreed to pay one hundred pounds to the family to pay for the trouble he had caused the girl. He obviously[6] did not like this agreement[7], so we were worried that he would try to escape and not pay.

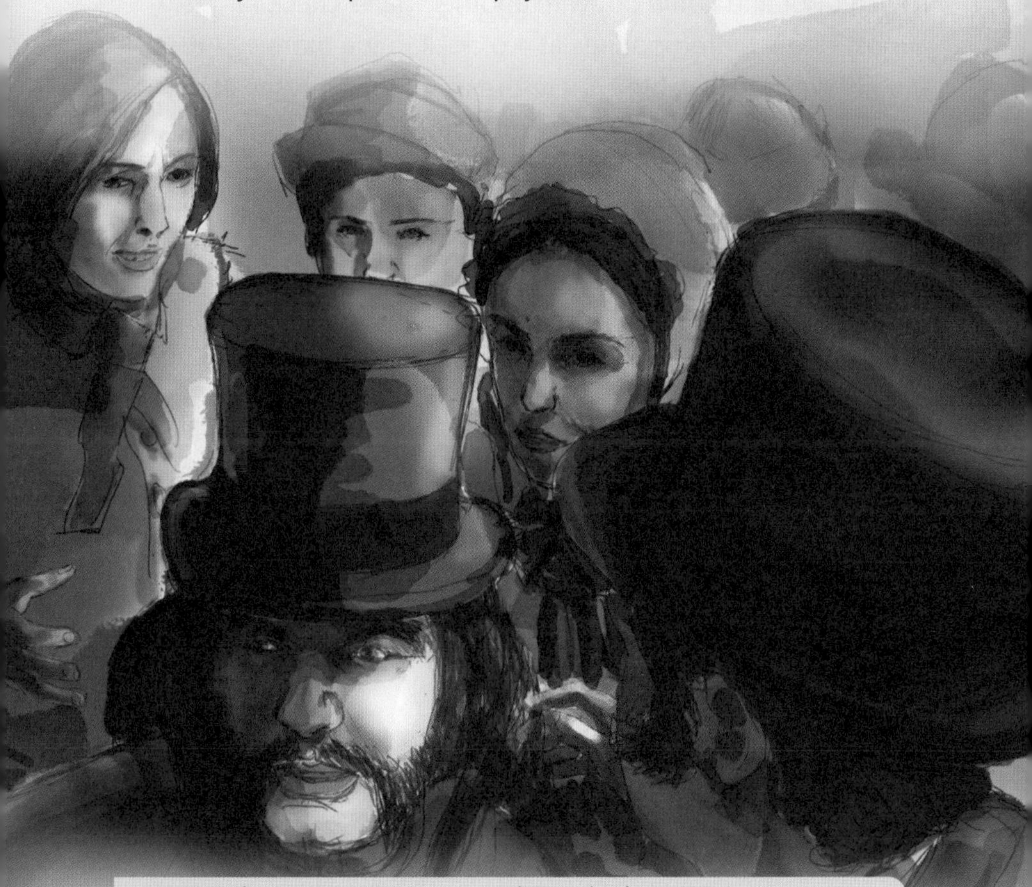

1 escape [ə`skep] (v.) 逃跑
2 expression [ɪk`sprɛʃən] (n.) 表情
3 protect [prə`tɛkt] (v.) 保護
4 attack [ə`tæk] (v.) 攻擊
5 demand [dɪ`mænd] (n.) 要求
6 obviously [`ɑbvɪəslɪ] (adv.) 顯然地
7 agreement [ə`grimənt] (n.) 同意；協定

8 "As he did not have that amount of money with him, he said he had to go and get a check[1]. And where do you think he went? He went to the house with the door we are looking at now, and came out with ten pounds in gold and a check for the rest. The check was signed[2] by a man whose name I cannot tell you, but he is a well-known and respectable person, and he is often in the news.

"I didn't trust him, and I told him so. Who can walk through such a door and come out with another man's check for almost one hundred pounds at 4 o'clock in the morning? It did not seem believable[3]. Therefore we made him stay at my house with the doctor, the girl's father and me until the banks opened in the morning. Then morning came, and after breakfast we went to cash the check. I handed it over myself and was sure that it would be a forgery[4], but to my surprise, it was genuine[5]."

Mr Utterson tut-tutted[6] when he heard this.

Trust

- What is trust? Write a definition.
- Think of a time when you trusted someone. Think of a time when you didn't trust someone. Tell a partner.

1 check [tʃɛk] (n.) 支票
2 sign [saɪn] (v.) 簽名
3 believable [bɪˋlivəbl̩] (a.) 可信的
4 forgery [ˋfɔrdʒərɪ] (n.) 偽造物
5 genuine [ˋdʒɛnjuɪn] (a.) 真的；非偽造的
6 tut-tut [ˋtʌtˋtʌt] (v.) 發嘖嘖聲

9

"I see you feel as I do," said Mr Enfield. "Yes, it's an unpleasant story. I don't think that any decent[7] person would want to be friendly with this man. Yet the man whose name was on the check is respectable, well-known and does good work in society. Perhaps he is an honest man who is being blackmailed[8] by this evil person for something he did wrong in his youth. But that doesn't explain everything."

"And do you know if this respectable person lives in this run-down[9] house?" asked a surprised Mr Utterson.

"No, I saw his address on the check. He lives at an address in a square somewhere else. In fact, I cannot understand how these two very different men are connected."

"Have you asked anyone about this?"

"No, I didn't want to stir up[10] trouble. 'Let sleeping dogs lie' is my motto[11]," said Mr Enfield.

"Yes, quite right. I agree," said the lawyer.

Let sleeping dogs lie

- What does this mean? Discuss in groups.
- Is there an equivalent expression in your first language?

7 decent [ˋdisn̩t] (a.) 正派的；像樣的
8 blackmail [ˋblæk͵mel] (v.) 敲詐；勒索
9 run-down [ˋrʌn͵daʊn] (a.) 失修的
10 stir up 激起
11 motto [ˋmɑto] (n.) 座右銘；格言

10 "It is a strange house, though," continued Mr Enfield. "Since that night I have studied it closely. There is no other door, and nobody uses the one that we can see except, occasionally[1], the man who knocked down the girl. The passage leads to a courtyard[2], and there are three windows that overlook the courtyard on the first floor[3], but none on the ground floor[4]. Someone must live there because the windows are always clean, although they are always shut, and there is usually smoke coming from the chimney. "

"That is a good rule of yours about sleeping dogs, Enfield, but there is one question I want to ask. What's the name of the man who knocked over the child?"

"Well, I suppose I can tell you. That very unpleasant person was a man by the name of Hyde," answered Mr Enfield.

"What does he look like?"

"He's not easy to describe[5]. There's something wrong, something unpleasant about his appearance, but it's hard to say exactly what it is. I never saw a man I disliked more. I really can't describe what's wrong with him. He just generally does not seem right. If I see him again, I will recognize[6] him, I am sure. It's just that I find it impossible to describe him in words."

"And you are sure he had a key for this door?" asked the lawyer.

"My dear sir . . .!" began Enfield.

1 occasionally [ə`keʒənl̩ɪ] (adv.) 偶爾
2 courtyard [`kort`jɑrd] (n.) 庭院；天井
3 the first floor〔英〕二樓
4 the ground floor〔英〕一樓
5 describe [dɪ`skraɪb] (v.) 描述；形容
6 recognize [`rɛkəg,naɪz] (v.) 承認；認出

11 "Yes, I know," said Utterson. "I know my questions seem strange, but you see I have not asked the name of the man who signed the check because I think I already know it. I need to be sure that you have told me the truth."

"I think you should have warned me," said Enfield unhappily.

"But I have told you the exact truth in every detail. Yes, he had a key. And what's more, I saw him use it again less than a week ago."

Mr Utterson stayed silent, but deep in thought.

"I made a mistake in talking about this. We will not talk about it again," said Mr Enfield.

"I completely agree," replied the lawyer. "Let us shake hands on it, Richard."

The Search for Mr Hyde

Mr Utterson lived alone. On Sundays he usually had his dinner and then he sat reading by the fire until midnight when the church bells rang and he would go gratefully[1] to bed. This evening he had his dinner as usual, but he could not forget about Enfield's story. After dinner, instead of reading, he went to the safe[2] in the room he used as his office and took out a document[3]. On the envelope were written the words: "Dr Jekyll's will"[4].

Mr Utterson had refused[5] to help in writing the will, though he was in charge of[6] it now that it had been written. The will stated[7] that if Dr Jekyll died, all his money and property[8] should go to "his friend, Edward Hyde". Also, if Dr Jekyll disappeared for any reason, or went absent without any explanation, after three months Mr Hyde would own all of Dr Jekyll's possessions[9].

1 gratefully [ˋgretfəlɪ] (adv.) 感恩地
2 safe [sef] (n.) 保險箱
3 document [ˋdakjəmənt] (n.) 公文；文件
4 will [wɪl] (n.) 遺囑

13

As a lawyer, Mr Utterson did not like this will at all, and now that he had heard the story about Mr Hyde, he liked it even less. He had previously thought it was foolish. Now he thought that there might be something bad involved[10].

He decided to go immediately to see his medical[11] friend Dr Lanyon, who might be able to tell him more. As soon as he arrived, Dr Lanyon welcomed him into the dining room, where he had been sitting alone drinking a glass of wine. The two men were old school and college friends. They respected each other and enjoyed each other's company.

After sitting and chatting[12] for a little while, Mr Utterson started talking about the subject that caused him to visit Lanyon that evening.

"I think we are Henry Jekyll's oldest friends," he said.

"Yes, I wish the friends were younger," Lanyon joked. "Why do you ask? I rarely see him these days."

"Why is that?" asked Utterson. "I thought you shared the same scientific interests."

"Yes, we do, or rather we used to[13]. We had a disagreement ten years ago and I think he began to go wrong," replied the doctor. "Of course I continue to take an interest in him, as an old friend, but his ideas became very unscientific. Absolute[14] rubbish[15], in fact!"

"Have you ever met a friend of his – someone called Hyde?" asked Mr Utterson aloud.

5 refuse [rɪ`fjuz] (v.) 拒絕；不肯
6 in charge of 負責
7 state [stet] (v.) 陳述
8 property [`prɑpɚtɪ] (n.) 財產
9 possessions [pə`zɛʃənz] (n.)〔複〕財產；所有物
10 involve [ɪn`vɑlv] (v.) 牽涉
11 medical [`mɛdɪkḷ] (a.) 醫學的；學醫的
12 chat [tʃæt] (v.) 聊天；閒談
13 used to [just tu] 過去時常做……
14 absolute [`æbsəˏlut] (a.) 純粹的；完全的
15 rubbish [`rʌbɪʃ] (n.) 垃圾；廢物

14 "No. Never heard of[1] him. He must have become a friend of Jekyll's after I stopped seeing him a lot," said Dr Lanyon.

After a few drinks and more conversation Mr Utterson returned home, but he found it difficult to sleep. He still could not forget about the story he had heard and the information[2] he had found out[3].

When the bells at the church next to his house struck[4] 6 o'clock in the morning, Utterson was still awake. Enfield's story was still going round[5] in his mind. He was worried about the hold[6] that Hyde seemed to have over his friend Dr Jekyll. He decided to try and find out more about the real Mr Hyde, hoping that he could then get to the heart of the mystery[7]. There might be a good reason for the strange will, and why Dr Jekyll was friends with the unpleasant Mr Hyde.

So from that day onwards[8], Mr Utterson often visited the street with the door.

"If he is Mr Hyde," he thought, with a smile, "I will be Mr Seek[9]."

Then, one cold, dry night his patience[10] was rewarded[11]. It was after 10 o'clock and all the shops were closed. The side street was empty and quiet, although the busy sounds of the city could be heard in the distance.

At that time of night, even quiet noises can carry a long way in the still air. Utterson heard some very light footsteps come near, and feeling that this was the man he was interested in, he moved back into the dark of the passage that led to the courtyard. He looked out carefully from the passage entrance and he saw a small, plainly dressed[12] man approach[13]. Even at a distance, Utterson knew he did not like him.

This man walked straight to the door, taking a key from his pocket. Mr Utterson stepped out of the darkness and touched the man's shoulder.

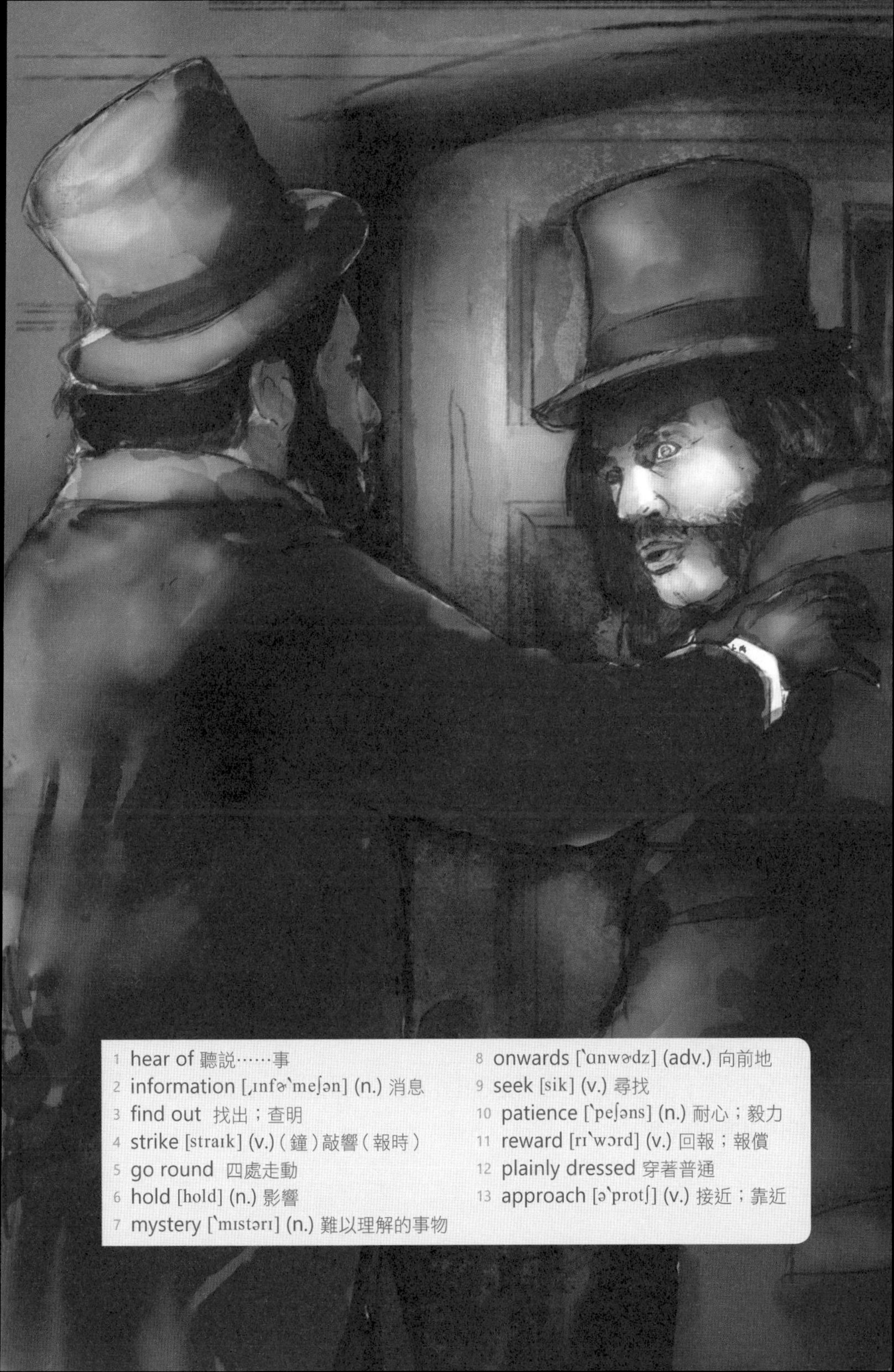

1 hear of 聽說……事
2 information [͵ɪnfɚˋmeʃən] (n.) 消息
3 find out 找出；查明
4 strike [straɪk] (v.)（鐘）敲響（報時）
5 go round 四處走動
6 hold [hold] (n.) 影響
7 mystery [ˋmɪstərɪ] (n.) 難以理解的事物
8 onwards [ˋɑnwɚdz] (adv.) 向前地
9 seek [sik] (v.) 尋找
10 patience [ˋpeʃəns] (n.) 耐心；毅力
11 reward [rɪˋwɔrd] (v.) 回報；報償
12 plainly dressed 穿著普通
13 approach [əˋprotʃ] (v.) 接近；靠近

"Excuse me," he said, "Mr Hyde, I believe?"

The man stepped back and appeared to grow smaller. "That is my name," he said quietly, not looking Utterson in the face. "What do you want?"

"I am Mr Utterson, an old friend of Dr Jekyll's, and since you are going into the house, I thought you could let me in too."

"Dr Jekyll is not here," replied the small man in a very unfriendly manner. "How do you know my name?"

"I will tell you, if you show me your face," said the lawyer.

At first Hyde did not move, but then he turned to face Mr Utterson. The two men stared at each other for several seconds.

"Now I will know you if I see you again," said Mr Utterson.

"Yes, it's good we have met, and I shall give you my address." He gave Mr Utterson the number of a street in Soho.

This surprised Utterson. "Is he thinking of the will?" he thought to himself. "Perhaps he is making sure I know where to find him so that he will receive Dr Jekyll's property easily." But he said nothing of this to Hyde.

"Now, how do you know me?" repeated Hyde.

"We have friends in common[1], and they have described you to me," said Mr Utterson.

"Who?" demanded[2] Hyde, suddenly[3] shouting loudly.

"Well, Dr Jekyll, for example."

"He never told you," said Hyde angrily. "I didn't think you would lie."

And very quickly, he unlocked the door and disappeared into the house.

Hyde's reaction

- Hyde seems to know that Utterson is not telling the truth. In pairs think of reasons why he knows that Dr Jekyll has not described Hyde to Utterson.

16

A puzzled[4] Mr Utterson stood still for a while. Then very slowly he began to walk away, frowning[5], and occasionally stopping, deep in thought. Yes, Mr Hyde was a very unpleasant and ugly-looking person, though it was not possible to point to any one feature[6] of his appearance that made him ugly. His voice was also unpleasant; it was rough[7] and broken. But there was something more, something that Mr Utterson could not immediately identify[8]. Perhaps it was just his unpleasant personality[9] that showed itself in his face and his behavior. There was definitely[10] something evil about Hyde, and Utterson felt worried that his friend Dr Jekyll had made a friend of Mr Hyde.

Just round the corner from the side street with the door, there was a square[11] of old, well-built houses, most of which were now divided into flats[12]. However, one house was still complete and kept as a single home. This was where Mr Utterson knocked at the door. An old, smartly dressed[13] servant opened it.

1 in common 共通的
2 demand [dɪ`mænd] (v.) 查問
3 suddenly [`sʌdn̩lɪ] (adv.) 突然地
4 puzzled [`pʌzl̩d] (a.) 困惑的
5 frown [fraʊn] (v.) 皺眉
6 feature [`fitʃɚ] (n.) 特徵
7 rough [rʌf] (a.) 粗糙的
8 identify [aɪ`dɛntə͵faɪ] (v.) 確認；識別
9 personality [͵pɝsn̩`ælətɪ] (n.) 人格；性格
10 definitely [`dɛfənɪtlɪ] (ad.) 明確地；清楚地
11 square [skwɛr] (n.) 街區
12 flat [flæt] (n.)〔英〕公寓
13 smartly dressed 衣著整潔

17 "Good evening, Poole. Is Dr Jekyll at home?" asked the lawyer.

"I will see, Mr Utterson. Will you come in, please?" said Poole.

Mr Utterson waited by the bright open fire in the very fine hall, perhaps his favorite room in London. But Mr Utterson couldn't help being very worried, and he was not looking forward to talking about it with his friend Dr Jekyll. When the servant returned to say that Dr Jekyll was not at home, Mr Utterson was not unhappy at the news.

"I saw Mr Hyde go in the back door round the corner," said the lawyer. "Is that normal when Dr Jekyll is not at home?"

"It is quite alright, Mr Utterson. Mr Hyde has a key," replied the servant.

"So Dr Jekyll trusts him, then?"

"Yes, indeed, sir, and we all have orders to obey[1] him. Though Mr Hyde is not often seen here on this side of the house, and he never stays to dinner. He usually comes and goes by that laboratory[2] door at the back."

"Well, goodnight then, Poole."

"Goodnight, Mr Utterson."

"Poor Henry Jekyll," thought Mr Utterson as he walked away. "He was wild in his youth, but I think he is now in an even more dangerous situation with Hyde. Perhaps Hyde has something to do with a shameful[3] event in Jekyll's past. Even if it was a long time ago, you can never escape some things. I expect Hyde himself has some terrible black secrets too. It makes me cold to think of this man stealing like a thief into Henry's life. I wonder how much Hyde knows about the will, and if he knows how easy it would be for him to inherit[4] Henry Jekyll's property. I must try and help, if Jekyll will let me."

1 obey [əˋbe] (v.) 遵守；聽從
2 laboratory [ˋlæbrə͵torɪ] (n.) 實驗室；研究室
3 shameful [ˋʃemfəl] (a.) 可恥的；丟臉的
4 inherit [ɪnˋhɛrɪt] (v.) 繼承

Dr Jekyll Was Quite at Ease

18 A fortnight later, Dr Jekyll gave one of his very pleasant dinners to half a dozen old friends, including Mr Utterson, who stayed on late after the others left. This was not the first time he had stayed late, and, as usual, the two friends sat in relaxed and contented[1] silence on either side of the fire. Now was Mr Utterson's chance to ask about Hyde and the will.

"I want to talk to you, Jekyll. You know that will of yours?" he said.

Dr Jekyll only hesitated[2] a moment before replying, apparently[3] cheerfully[4]. "You have a poor client[5] in me, I'm afraid. You have never liked that will, I know. The only man who I have upset more than I have upset[6] you is Dr Lanyon." It seemed Jekyll was trying to change the subject. "He has never agreed with my scientific ideas. I am very disappointed[7] with him."

"Well you know I have doubts about that will," said Utterson, ignoring[8] the mention of Dr Lanyon.

"Yes, you've told me before," said Jekyll rather sharply.

"Well, I'm telling you again, because I have found out something about Mr Hyde recently."

Dr Jekyll's face lost its smile and he became very pale[9]. "I thought we had agreed not to talk about this."

"But I have heard something very bad."

"That doesn't matter. You do not understand my situation," said Dr Jekyll quietly. "It cannot be solved[10] by talking."

19

"You can trust me, Jekyll. You know that. Please tell me what's going on."

"This is very good of you, Utterson, and yes, I trust you more than any other man alive. It's not as bad as perhaps you think. Just so you can stop worrying I will tell you one thing. I will tell you this: I can be free of Mr Hyde at any time I wish. I promise you this. Thank you very much for your concern[11], but I beg you, please, this is a private[12] matter. Do not speak of it, and don't even think of it again."

Mr Utterson was silent, looking into the fire. At last he said, "Yes, I am sure you are absolutely right," and he got to his feet, ready to leave.

"As you have mentioned him, and as I hope never to talk about it again, let me just say that I have a great interest in poor Mr Hyde," said Jekyll. "He told me that you saw him, and he told me what happened. I am afraid he was rude[13]. But I would like you to promise me that you will help him get his rights. I would be much happier if you promised that."

"Well," sighed Mr Utterson, "I certainly can't pretend[14] that I will ever like him, but, very well, Henry, I promise."

1 contented [kən`tɛntɪd] (a.) 知足的
2 hesitate [`hɛzə,tet] (v.) 躊躇；猶豫
3 apparently [ə`pærəntlɪ] (adv.) 顯然地
4 cheerfully [`tʃɪrfəlɪ] (adv.) 興高采烈地
5 client [`klaɪənt] (n.) 委託人；客戶
6 upset [ʌp`sɛt] (v.) 使心煩
7 disappointed [,dɪsə`pɔɪntɪd] (a.) 失望的
8 ignore [ɪg`nor] (v.) 忽視；不理會
9 pale [pel] (a.) 蒼白的；暗淡的
10 solve [sɑlv] (v.) 解決；解答
11 concern [kən`sɝn] (n.) 關心
12 private [`praɪvɪt] (a.) 私人的
13 rude [rud] (a.) 粗魯的；野蠻的
14 pretend [prɪ`tɛnd] (v.) 假裝；佯稱

The Carew Murder Case

20 About a year later, in October, a very important man, a Member of Parliament[1], was horribly murdered[2] in London. The crime[3] was seen by a servant girl who was looking out of her window at about 11 o'clock one moonlit night. She saw a tall, old, white-haired gentleman walking along the street and a smaller man coming from the opposite[4] direction.

When they met under her window, she saw the older man bow[5]. Then she heard him speak to the other man. She recognized the other man as Mr Hyde, a man who had once visited her employer[6]. Although the tall man's greeting seemed quite friendly, and might have been a polite[7] request for directions, the smaller man flew into a violent[8] temper[9], and started hitting the white-haired gentleman with a thick walking-stick.

21 He repeatedly hit him, "like a madman[10]" as the servant said, until the older man fell to the ground. Then Hyde started kicking and stamping on him. The servant heard the sound of breaking bones and then she fainted[11].

It was 2 o'clock when she woke up again and called for the police. Hyde had gone, but the broken body of the tall old man was still lying on the ground. The stick that Hyde had used had broken in half in the violent action, and one of the pieces was lying near the body. The other half had been carried away by the murderer. When the police arrived, they found money and a gold watch in the old man's pockets, and also an envelope addressed to Mr Utterson.

The envelope was taken to the lawyer at his home early in the morning, before he got out of bed. Mr Utterson would say nothing until he saw the body. There he recognized the body as that of Sir Danvers Carew, the well-known and well-respected Member of Parliament.

The police now realized that this was a very important case and asked Utterson to help them find the criminal[12]. They told him what the servant had seen, and the name by which she knew the murderer. At the mention of Hyde's name, Utterson grew frightened. Then they showed him the broken walking-stick. Mr Utterson recognized it as a part of a walking-stick that he had given Dr Jekyll many years ago. It was clear that the "Mr Hyde" the servant had seen was the same Mr Hyde that he knew.

1 Parliament [ˋpɑrləmənt] (n.) 國會
2 murder [ˋmɝdɚ] (v.) 謀殺；兇殺
3 crime [kraɪm] (n.) 罪行
4 opposite [ˋɑpəzɪt] (a.) 對面的
5 bow [baʊ] (v.) 鞠躬
6 employer [ɪmˋplɔɪɚ] (n.) 雇主
7 polite [pəˋlaɪt] (a.) 禮貌的
8 violent [ˋvaɪələnt] (a.) 暴力的
9 fly into a temper 發脾氣
10 madman [ˋmædmən] (n.) 瘋子
11 faint [fent] (v.) 昏厥；暈倒
12 criminal [ˋkrɪmən!] (n.) 罪犯

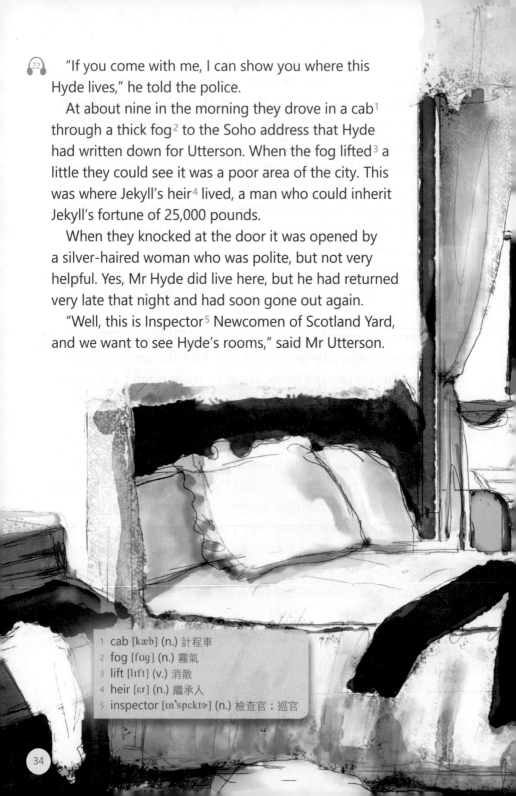

"If you come with me, I can show you where this Hyde lives," he told the police.

At about nine in the morning they drove in a cab[1] through a thick fog[2] to the Soho address that Hyde had written down for Utterson. When the fog lifted[3] a little they could see it was a poor area of the city. This was where Jekyll's heir[4] lived, a man who could inherit Jekyll's fortune of 25,000 pounds.

When they knocked at the door it was opened by a silver-haired woman who was polite, but not very helpful. Yes, Mr Hyde did live here, but he had returned very late that night and had soon gone out again.

"Well, this is Inspector[5] Newcomen of Scotland Yard, and we want to see Hyde's rooms," said Mr Utterson.

1 cab [kæb] (n.) 計程車
2 fog [fɑg] (n.) 霧氣
3 lift [lɪft] (v.) 消散
4 heir [ɛr] (n.) 繼承人
5 inspector [ɪnˋspɛktɚ] (n.) 檢查官；巡官

"Oh, is he in trouble?" said the woman with an evil-looking grin[1] on her face. "What has he done?"

"Just let us have a look inside," said the Inspector.

"No-one seems to like Hyde," he said quietly to Utterson.

When they were inside, they found that Hyde only used two of the many rooms in the house. But these rooms, they saw, were very well-furnished[2] and even luxurious. They also saw that the two rooms had very recently been searched by someone in a great hurry. Drawers[3] were left open and their contents[4] thrown around the rooms. Clothes lay all over the floor, with their pockets inside out.

There was also a pile of ashes[5] in the cold fireplace[6], in which Newcomen found the remains[7] of a check book. There was also a broken half of a walking-stick leaning against the wall behind the door. The stick, Inspector Newcomen decided, proved[8] that Hyde was the murderer.

24

Because he found the check book in the ashes, he also decided to visit Hyde's bank. When they reached the bank and talked to the manager, they discovered that there were several thousand pounds in Hyde's account[9].

"Now we know we can find him easily," said the Inspector. "He must have lost his mind otherwise he would never have been stupid enough to burn the check book and then leave the stick for us to find. Why[10], money is life to the man. All we have to do is wait for him at the bank, and let everyone know we are looking for him," said the policeman.

However, this was easier said than done. Very few people knew anything about Hyde, and no-one had any photographs[11] of him. His family could not be found, and no-one could agree on an exact description[12] of him, except that in some indescribable[13] and haunting[14] way he did not look normal.

1 grin [grɪn] (v.) (n.) 露齒而笑
2 well-furnished [ˋwɛlˋfɝnɪʃt] (a.) 裝潢漂亮的
3 drawer [ˋdrɔɚ] (n.) 抽屜
4 contents [ˋkɑntɛnts] (n.)〔複〕內容物
5 ashes [ˋæʃɪz] (n.)〔複〕灰燼
6 fireplace [ˋfaɪr͵ples] (n.) 壁爐
7 remains [rɪˋmenz] (n.)〔複〕剩餘物
8 prove [pruv] (v.) 證明
9 account [əˋkaʊnt] (n.) 帳戶
10 why [hwaɪ] (int.) 唔；當然
11 photograph [ˋfotə͵græf] (n.) 相片
12 description [dɪˋskrɪpʃən] (n.) 形容
13 indescribable [͵ɪndɪˋskraɪbəbl̩] (a.) 難以形容的
14 haunting [ˋhɔntɪŋ] (a.) 縈繞於心頭的

The Incident of the Letter

25 Late that afternoon, Mr Utterson went to Dr Jekyll's house again. The servant Poole let him in and led him through the house and across the back garden to the building at the back which Dr Jekyll had made into a laboratory.

It was the first time that Utterson had seen the laboratory, which he noticed was windowless[1] and seemed to him rather dirty. Chemistry equipment[2] and large boxes were scattered[3] all around the place. At the end of the room, there was a flight of stairs[4] leading to a red door, which led to Dr Jekyll's private office.

This was a large room with cupboards[5], a large mirror, a fire and a lamp. Three locked windows looked out onto a courtyard. Utterson saw Dr Jekyll sitting near the fire, looking sick. Jekyll held out a cold hand, and welcomed Utterson in a weak voice.

"Have you heard the news about the murder?" asked Mr Utterson as soon as Poole had left.

"Yes, I heard people outside shouting about it. I heard them from my dining room."

"Carew was my client," said Utterson, "but so are you. I want to know how this might affect[6] me, so I must ask if you have been stupid enough to hide this murderer, Mr Hyde."

1 windowless [ˋwɪndolɪs] (a.) 沒有窗戶的
2 equipment [ɪˋkwɪpmənt] (n.) 設備
3 scatter [ˋskætɚ] (v.) 散佈
4 a flight of stairs 一段階梯
5 cupboard [ˋkʌbɚd] (n.) 壁櫥
6 affect [əˋfɛkt] (v.) 影響
7 sincerely [sɪnˋsɪrlɪ] (adv.) 由衷地
8 advice [ədˋvaɪs] (n.) 忠告
9 upright [ˋʌp͵raɪt] (a.) 挺直的

"I swear to God I will never see him again. I am finished with him, I promise," said the doctor. "It is all over. "

"I sincerely[7] hope you are right," said the lawyer.

"There is something I need your advice[8] about," said Jekyll. "I have received a letter, but I don't know if I should show it to the police or not. I trust you, so I'd like to give the letter to you and let you decide what to do with it."

Jekyll handed a sheet of paper over to Utterson. The letter was written in a strange upright[9] style, and was signed by Hyde. It said that Dr Jekyll, who had been so good to him, and to whom Hyde had never been grateful enough, was in no danger from him and that he, Hyde, had a sure means of escape.

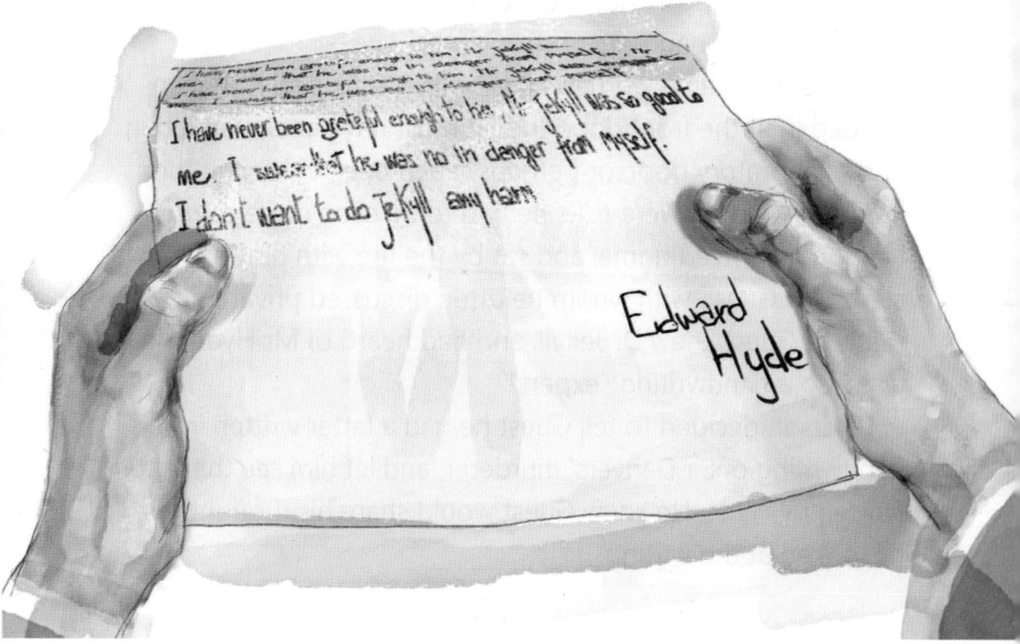

Utterson felt a little better after reading this. It seemed that Hyde did not want to do his friend Jekyll any harm[1] after all. Perhaps his earlier doubts about Hyde were not all correct.

"Do you have the envelope?" asked Utterson.

"Er, no, I burnt it before I realized it was important. But it had no postmark[2] – it was handed in[3] at the door."

"I will think about what to do with this," said Utterson. "Tell me, was it Hyde who made you write that paragraph[4] in your will about what happens if you disappear?"

Dr Jekyll was silent, but nodded[5] his head. "What a lesson I have had!" he exclaimed[6].

"I thought so. He meant to murder you. You are lucky to have escaped."

As Mr Utterson left, he asked Poole if anyone had handed in a letter earlier that day. But Poole said he was sure that no letter had been handed in.

Utterson became worried again. If the letter had not been handed in at the front door, then it must have been handed in at the laboratory door, or perhaps it had been written in the laboratory. If that were true, he had to be even more careful.

Soon he arrived home, and sat by the fire with his head[7] clerk[8], Mr Guest, with whom he often discussed private matters. Guest knew Dr Jekyll, and had heard of Mr Hyde. He was also a handwriting[9] expert[10].

Utterson decided to tell Guest he had a letter written in the handwriting of Sir Danvers' murderer, and let him see the letter written by Hyde. He knew Guest would share his thoughts as he looked at the writing.

28

"Yes, it is a sad business about Sir Danvers Carew's murder. The murderer must be mad, of course," said Guest.

"Well, I'd like to hear your views on that. I have a document here in the murderer's handwriting," said Utterson. "There it is: a murderer's autograph[11]."

Guest sat down at once and studied it with passion.

"Well, it's a strange style of writing, Mr Utterson. But, no, I do not think the writer is mad," he said.

"Yes, and by all accounts[12] a very strange writer," added Utterson.

At that moment Utterson's servant came in with a note from Dr Jekyll inviting Utterson to dinner.

"May I see that note?" said Guest. "Thank you. That's interesting. The handwriting in the letter and the note are very similar. It is only the slope[13] that varies."

"Well, that's a surprising coincidence[14]," said Utterson.

"Yes, quite a coincidence," agreed Guest.

"I wouldn't say anything to anyone about this note, Guest."

"No, of course not, sir. I understand."

Later, Utterson locked the note away and wondered why Jekyll had written it in Hyde's name. "Why would he forge[15] for a murderer?" he thought. And the blood ran cold in his veins[16].

1 do sb harm 傷害某人
2 postmark [ˋpost,mɑrk] (n.) 郵戳
3 hand in 繳交
4 paragraph [ˋpærə,græf] (n.) 文章的段或節
5 nod [nɑd] (v.) 點頭
6 exclaim [ɪksˋklem] (v.) 叫喊著說出
7 head [hɛd] (a.) 首要的
8 clerk [klɝk] (n.) 職員
9 handwriting [ˋhænd,raɪtɪŋ] (n.) 筆跡
10 expert [ˋɛkspɚt] (n.) 專家
11 autograph [ˋɔtə,græf] (n.) 親筆簽名；親筆稿
12 by all accounts 根據各種流傳的說法
13 slope [slop] (n.) 斜度
14 coincidence [koˋɪnsɪdəns] (n.) 巧合
15 forge [fɔrdʒ] (v.) 偽造
16 vein [ven] (n.) 血管

The Remarkable Incident of Dr Lanyon

29 The murder of Sir Danvers Carew was big news in the city. Sir Danvers was very well respected so his murder made many people very angry. A large reward[1] of several thousand pounds was offered[2] to anyone who could tell the police where Hyde was, but no-one knew. Hyde had completely disappeared.

After a while life began to return to normal for Mr Utterson. The sadness of the loss[3] of Sir Danvers was balanced[4] by the satisfaction of the loss of Hyde. It seemed definite now that the evil Hyde had disappeared.

Life was also becoming better for Dr Jekyll. He went out, was busy, dined[5] with friends, and for about two months he seemed to be happy and content.

On 8th January, Jekyll and Utterson dined with their friend Dr Lanyon, and all seemed well again between the three, just like in the old days. Utterson was used to going round to see his friend Jekyll almost daily. So the following day he decided to return once more to visit his friend. But he did not get in to see him. Poole told Utterson at the door that the doctor was staying indoors, and would see nobody.

He tried again several times to see his friend, and was again refused. On the sixth night Mr Utterson went to see Dr Lanyon instead.

There, things were not much better. Although he was not kept at the door, when he went in he was shocked at Lanyon's pale appearance and his obvious general weakness. Lanyon looked as though he was near death. He was thinner, balder[6] and looked much older. He had a frightened look in his eyes.

"I have had a terrible shock and I will never recover[7]," said Lanyon.

"Jekyll is ill too. Have you seen him?" said Utterson.

"I wish to hear or see nothing more of that man! Please do not mention him!" exclaimed Lanyon.

Mr Utterson was silent for a while, then he said, "Is there nothing I can do? We are three very old friends. We may not live long enough to make others."

"Nothing can be done. Absolutely nothing. Ask Jekyll."

"He will not see me," replied Utterson.

"I'm not surprised at that," said Lanyon. "After I am dead, you may find out what has happened. I cannot tell you now. Please talk about something else if you wish to stay. But if you cannot leave this subject alone, then please go!"

Later, when he arrived home, Utterson sat down and wrote a letter to Jekyll asking why he would not see him, and why he and Lanyon were no longer friends. A long, rather strange reply came from Jekyll the following day.

1 reward [rɪ`wɔrd] (n.) 懸賞獎金
2 offer [`ɔfɚ] (v.) 提供
3 loss [lɔs] (n.) 喪失；損失
4 balance [`bæləns] (v.) 平衡
5 dine [daɪn] (v.) 進餐；宴請
6 bald [bɔld] (a.) 禿頭的
7 recover [rɪ`kʌvɚ] (v.) 恢復

31 Jekyll did not blame[1] Lanyon, he wrote, but agreed they should never meet. He said he had done a great wrong, and would no longer see people. He would not discuss the reasons, and from now on he would lead a life of seclusion[2]. He wrote that Utterson was still his friend but Utterson should not be surprised if Jekyll's door was shut to him. He, Jekyll, had done a great wrong and had to suffer[3] the punishment[4]. He asked Utterson to respect his wishes.

Mr Utterson was amazed[5]. The evil Hyde had gone, everything seemed to be going well, and Jekyll had seemed very happy. But now he wondered why everything had changed for the worse within the last week.

A week afterwards Dr Lanyon stopped getting up, and in less than a fortnight[6] he was dead. The night after the funeral[7] Mr Utterson locked himself in his office and very sadly took out Lanyon's will. The large envelope had the words: 'PRIVATE: for the hands of J.G. Utterson ALONE and in case of[8] his death *to be destroyed[9] unread.*'

Within the large outer envelope there was another envelope with these words written on the front: 'Not to be opened till the death or disappearance of Dr Henry Jekyll.'

Mr Utterson could not believe his eyes. Yes, the word was 'disappearance' and again it was linked to the name of Dr Jekyll! This was very like Jekyll's own will, which Utterson had long ago returned to him. The idea of Jekyll's disappearance (and Utterson had not seen Jekyll for a long time) reminded him of the terrible Mr Hyde.

1 blame [blem] (v.) 責備
2 seclusion [sɪˋkluʒən] (n.) 與世隔絕
3 suffer [ˋsʌfɚ] (v.) 遭受
4 punishment [ˋpʌnɪʃmənt] (n.) 懲罰
5 amazed [əˋmezd] (n.) 吃驚的
6 fortnight [ˋfɔrt͵naɪt] (n.) 兩星期
7 funeral [ˋfjunərəl] (n.) 出殯
8 in case of 如果發生
9 destroy [dɪˋstrɔɪ] (v.) 銷毀

32

What was going on? Why had Lanyon written this? Utterson was a lawyer and had to keep the secrets people gave him, and follow the rules they set[1]. Now he felt like breaking this rule[2], and opening the envelope, but eventually[3] he kept to his professional[4] standards[5] and he returned his dead friend's will to the secrecy[6] of his safe.

He continued to try to see Jekyll from time to time[7], but was perhaps relieved[8] when Dr Jekyll's servant Poole would not let him in. In his heart, perhaps, he preferred to[9] speak with Poole on the doorstep rather than enter Jekyll's voluntary[10] prison[11].

Poole told Utterson that the doctor kept to his office above the laboratory more than ever, and would even sleep there sometimes. Dr Jekyll was unhappy, usually silent, and did not even read. Poole's reports were always the same, so, over time, Mr Utterson visited less and less[12].

1 set [sɛt] (v.) 訂定；規定
2 break the rule 打破規則
3 eventually [ɪ`vɛntʃuəlɪ] (adv.) 最後地；終於地
4 professional [prə`fɛʃənḷ] (a.) 職業的
5 standard [`stændɚd] (n.) 規範
6 secrecy [`sikrəsɪ] (n.) 祕密狀態
7 from time to time 不時；偶爾
8 relieved [rɪ`livd] (a.) 鬆口氣的
9 prefer to 寧可……
10 voluntary [`vɑlən,tɛrɪ] (a.) 自願的；自發的
11 prison [`prɪzṇ] (n.) 監獄
12 less and less 愈來愈少的

The Incident at the Window

(33) One Sunday, Mr Utterson was taking his regular[1] walk with Mr Enfield. They were strolling once again along the side street. When they arrived in front of the door they both stopped to look at it. Mr Enfield said, "Well, at least that story's at an end. We'll never see Hyde again, thank God."

"I hope not," said Utterson. "Did I ever tell you I saw him once, and shared your feeling of disgust[2] about him?"

"That happens with everyone. You can't see him without feeling that," said Enfield. "By the way, you must have thought I was a fool not to realize this door was the back door to Dr Jekyll's house."

"So you found that out, did you?" said Utterson. "In that case, as we are here, let's go through the passage into the courtyard to see if we can see Jekyll at the windows."

The courtyard was cool and quite dark, even though the day was sunny. At the half-open middle window on the first floor[3], they looked up and saw Dr Jekyll sitting with a sad face, gazing[4] out into the courtyard.

34

"Hello there, Jekyll!" shouted Mr Utterson. "I trust you are better."

"I am not well," replied Jekyll, "not well at all. It will not last long, thank God."

"You stay indoors too much," said the lawyer. "You should be out, like my cousin here, Mr Enfield, and me. Let me introduce you – Mr Enfield, Dr Jekyll – Dr Jekyll, Mr Enfield."

They nodded to each other.

"Come on, Henry. Get your hat and coat and come for a short walk with us."

"You are very good, and it's a pleasure to see you both. I would very much like to come for a walk with you, but it's quite impossible. I dare not[5]. I would like to ask you and Mr Enfield in, but the house is not fit[6] for visitors."

"Well, then, we can talk to you from here!" shouted the lawyer with a smile.

1 regular [ˋrɛgjələ] (a.) 定期的；一般的
2 disgust [dɪsˋgʌst] (n.) 厭惡
3 the first floor〔英〕二樓
4 gaze [gez] (v.) 注視
5 I dare not 我不敢；我最好不要
6 fit [fɪt] (a.) 適合的

35 "That's exactly what I was going to suggest," said Jekyll, also smiling.

But as soon as he had spoken these words, the smile left his face and was replaced by an expression of terror[1] that froze[2] the blood of the two friends down below in the courtyard. Suddenly Dr Jekyll slammed[3] the window shut[4] and they could see him no more.

Both Utterson and Enfield were shocked and silent as they walked away through the passage and along the side street. It was some time before they arrived at a busier part of the town and Mr Utterson exclaimed, "God forgive[5] us!"

Mr Enfield replied only with a serious expression and a nod, and they walked on in sad silence.

Utterson

- Imagine you meet Utterson. What questions would you ask him? With a partner ask questions and decide Utterson's answers.

1 terror [ˋtɛrɚ] (n.) 恐怖；驚駭
2 freeze [friz] (v.) 結冰；凝固
3 slam [slæm] (v.) 猛地關上
4 shut [ʃʌt] (a.) 關閉的
5 forgive [fɚˋgɪv] (v.) 原諒
6 can't take it any more 無法再忍受了
7 support [səˋport] (v.) 支持；證明
8 wicked [ˋwɪkɪd] (a.) 缺德的

The Last Night

36 Mr Utterson was sitting by his fire at home one evening after dinner when he was surprised to receive a visit from Dr Jekyll's servant Poole.

"Bless me Poole, what brings you here?" cried Utterson. "Is the doctor ill?"

"Mr Utterson," said the man. "There is something wrong."

"Sit down, Poole, and have a glass of wine. Now, take your time and tell me slowly and clearly what has happened."

"You know the doctor's ways, sir," replied Poole, "and how he shuts himself away in his office, sir. Well, he's shut himself away in his office again, and I don't like it. I'm afraid."

"What do you mean, Poole? What are you afraid of?"

"It's been like this for about a week, sir," said Poole, not answering Utterson's question. "I can't take it any more[6]!"

Poole's appearance supported[7] his words. He sat looking helpless, staring into the corner, his wine untouched, not looking the lawyer in the face.

"Come on now, I can see there's something seriously wrong. Try to tell me what it is," said Utterson.

"I dare not say, but I think something wicked[8] has happened," said Poole in a frightened voice. "Will you please come and see for yourself, sir?"

37 Mr Utterson quickly fetched[1] his coat and hat. He noted the grateful expression on Poole's face, and the fact that Poole had still not touched the glass of wine.

The two men walked rapidly[2] through the cold and windy London night. The moon was pale and the streets were unusually empty of people, but full of wind and dust[3]. It was a bad night to be outside.

When they reached Dr Jekyll's house, Poole stopped in the middle of the pavement[4] and said, with a frightened voice, "Well, here we are, sir, and I hope nothing is wrong."

Poole knocked carefully and the door was opened on the chain by a frightened female servant. "Is that you, Poole?" she whispered[5].

"It's alright," said Poole, "You can open the door."

In the hall a large number of Dr Jekyll's servants were standing together in front of the bright fire like a flock[6] of sheep, all looking very worried.

"Thank God, it's Mr Utterson!" cried the cook, and ran forward as if[7] to take him in her arms.

"What's going on? What are you all doing here?" cried Utterson. "This is all very unusual. What would Dr Jekyll say?"

"They're all afraid," said Poole. "Please follow me, Mr Utterson," and Poole took a candle and led him into the back garden and towards the laboratory.

"Now please be very quiet and don't let him know you are here," said Poole. "Please listen, but don't speak. And if by chance[8] he asks you into his office, don't go!"

38

With that, a very surprised Utterson followed Poole into the laboratory and to the foot of the stairs at the far end. Poole left Utterson there and, clearly frightened, slowly walked up the stairs to the door.

"Mr Utterson is here, asking to see you, sir," he said to the closed door.

"Tell him I cannot see anyone," answered a complaining[9] voice from behind the door.

"Thank you, sir," replied Poole, who seemed very satisfied[10] with this answer, and led Mr Utterson back through the garden to the large kitchen of the main house.

When they got there, Poole looked into Utterson's eyes and asked very seriously, "Sir, was that my employer's voice?"

"Well, it seemed very changed," replied Utterson, very pale, but looking Poole in the eyes.

"I have worked for Dr Jekyll for twenty years. I don't think I am wrong if I say that is not his voice. I think the doctor has been killed; I believe he was killed eight days ago. We heard him cry out. Now, who – or what – is there inside the office instead of him? And why does this . . . this thing . . . stay there? That's what we want to know!"

"This is a very strange story," said Utterson. "And a very wild story, Poole. If – and I only say if – Dr Jekyll has been, well, murdered, why has the murderer stayed there? It doesn't make sense[11]."

1 fetch [fɛtʃ] (v.) 拿來
2 rapidly [ˋræpɪdlɪ] (adv.) 很快地
3 dust [dʌst] (n.) 灰塵；塵土
4 pavement [ˋpevmənt] (n.) 人行道
5 whisper [ˋhwɪspɚ] (v.) 低聲說
6 flock [flɑk] (n.) 畜群；人群
7 as if 猶如
8 by chance 意外地
9 complaining [kəmˋplenɪŋ] (a.) 發牢騷的
10 satisfied [ˋsætɪs͵faɪd] (a.) 感到滿意的
11 make sense 有意義；有道理

39

"Mr Utterson," said Poole, "you are a difficult man to persuade[1], but I'll try. Whoever or whatever is in that office has been there for a week, crying out for some kind of medicine. Sometimes Dr Jekyll would write instructions[2] on a piece of paper and leave it on the stairs. This week we've had nothing else – only a closed door and pieces of paper with instructions written on them and thrown[3] onto the stairs. Two or three times a day I have been sent running to all the chemists[4]' shops in the town. As soon as I returned from one with the drug[5] he wants, there would be another paper telling me to return it because it is not pure, and telling me to go to a different chemist. The drug is wanted very much, sir, whatever he wants it for."

"Have you kept any of these notes?" asked Utterson.

Poole reached into a pocket and handed him a crumpled[6] up piece of paper. This contained a message to a chemist asking for the "old pure drug" to be supplied[7], "at any price." At the end, the calm nature of the message became quite wild and the writer finished with, 'For God's sake[8], find me some of the old drug!'

"Very strange," said Utterson, quietly. Then much more sharply[9], "Why is it not sealed[10]? Why do you have an opened message?"

"The chemist was very angry, sir, and threw it back at me, so I picked it up and brought it back."

"Are you sure this is the doctor's writing?" said Utterson.

1 persuade [pə`swed] (v.) 說服
2 instruction [ɪn`strʌkʃən] (n.) 指示
3 throw [θro] (v.) 丟；扔
4 chemist [`kɛmɪst] (n.)〔英〕藥劑師
5 drug [drʌg] (n.) 藥
6 crumple [`krʌmp!] (v.) 弄皺
7 supply [sə`plaɪ] (v.) 供應
8 for God's sake 搞什麼名堂（帶著不滿的語氣）
9 sharply [`ʃɑrplɪ] (adv.) 語氣尖銳地
10 seal [sil] (v.) 密封

40

"I thought it looked like it, but it doesn't matter[1] whether it is or not, because I saw him!"

"You saw him?" repeated Utterson. "Well?"

"Yes, I went suddenly into the laboratory from the garden one day and saw him on the stairs. He had come out of the office for a moment[2]. He looked up and gave a kind of cry, and quickly ran back into the office. I only saw him for a second[3], but the sight of him made my hair stand on end[4]! If that was my employer, he must have had a mask[5] on his face, because his face looked completely different! And if it was him, why did he cry out and run away from me back into the office? I have worked for him for so many years."

"This is all very strange indeed," said Utterson, "but I'm beginning to see what might have happened. I think your employer Dr Jekyll could have a very painful[6] illness which also affects his appearance. That would explain him crying out, and it would also explain why he does not want his friends to see him. It might explain the change in his voice too, and being so desperate[7] to buy the right drug so that he can get well again."

"Sir," said Poole, stubbornly[8], "that thing is not my employer. That's the truth. Dr Jekyll is a tall fine man, but this one was small and ugly."

Poole continued, "I'm sure it's not him. Don't you think I know my own employer after seeing him every morning for twenty years? Don't you think I know how tall he is? No, that thing in the mask is not Dr Jekyll. I think the doctor has been murdered."

1 it doesn't matter 那不要緊
2 for a moment 片刻
3 for a second 一下下的時間
4 make somebody's hair stand on end 把某人嚇得汗毛直豎
5 mask [mæsk] (n.) 面具

Dr Jekyll

- What do you think has happened to Dr Jekyll? Discuss with a partner.

41

"If you think that, Poole, I have to make certain. This note suggests Jekyll is still alive. It is my duty to break into[9] the office and find out the truth."

"Yes," cried Poole, "yes – that's what to do!"

"So who is going to do it?" asked Utterson.

"Why, you and me, sir," replied Poole immediately.

"I've got an axe[10]," continued Poole. "And you may want to take the kitchen poker[11] for yourself."

Mr Utterson picked up the poker. "Poole," he said, "you and I are about to place ourselves in a position[12] of some danger. We should be frank[13]. We are both thinking more than we are saying. This masked figure you saw, did you recognize it?"

"It was so quick I could not be sure, but if you are asking if it was Mr Hyde, well, yes, I think it was. He was about the same size, and who else can have got in by the laboratory door? Mr Hyde still had the key at the time of the murder. And that's not all. Have you ever seen Hyde, Mr Utterson?"

"Yes, I spoke to him once."

"Then you must know that there is something strange about him – something frightening and terrible."

"Yes, I felt something like that too."

6 painful [ˋpenfəl] (a.) 疼痛的；痛苦
7 desperate [ˋdɛspərɪt] (a.) 情急拼命的
8 stubbornly [ˋstʌbənlɪ] (adv.) 倔強地
9 break into 闖入
10 axe [æks] (n.) 斧頭
11 poker [ˋpokɚ] (n.) 撥火棒；火鉗
12 position [pəˋzɪʃən] (n.) 位置
13 frank [fræŋk] (a.) 坦白的

42

"Exactly, sir. When I saw that thing, that's what I felt. I felt my spine[1] turn to ice. I swear it was Mr Hyde!"

"I thought so," said Utterson. "I think perhaps poor Henry has been killed, and his murderer is still there in that room. Well, let's see if we are right."

They called for two servants to go round to the back door to make sure no-one escaped that way. Utterson told them that Poole and he would wait ten minutes to allow them to reach their position.

At this Utterson said, "And now, Poole, let's get to our position."

He led Poole across the garden and towards the laboratory. It was now very dark and quiet. The wind blew[2] the flame[3] of the candle, throwing their shadows[4] around the garden. It was so quiet they could hear the soft footsteps[5] of the man walking to and fro in the office.

"Those are not the footsteps of Dr Jekyll," said Utterson. "They are too light."

"It's been walking up and down like that all day," said Poole, "and only stops when a new sample of the drug arrives."

"Is there anything else you can tell me?" asked Utterson.

Poole nodded. "Yes, once I heard it weeping[6] like a woman, or a lost soul[7]. It was a terrible sound. It made me feel like crying too."

By then, ten minutes had passed. Poole picked up the axe and they very quietly approached the door, holding their breath.

"Jekyll!" shouted Mr Utterson, "I demand to see you!"

1 spine [spaɪn] (n.) 脊柱；脊椎
2 blow [blo] (v.) 吹
3 flame [flem] (n.) 火焰
4 shadow [ˋʃædo] (n.) 影子
5 footstep [ˋfʊt͵stɛp] (n.) 腳步聲
6 weep [wip] (v.) 哭泣
7 soul [sol] (n.) 靈魂

He waited for a moment, but there was no reply.

"I am warning you," he shouted again, "I must see you and I shall see you. If you do not open the door yourself, then we will break the door down[1]!"

"Utterson, please have mercy[2]!" said the voice in reply.

"That's not Jekyll's voice," said Utterson to Poole. "It's Hyde's!"

Then they attacked the door. Poole swung[3] the axe over his shoulder and the blow he struck was so strong that it could be felt throughout the building. But the door was only knocked backwards a little. Poole swung again and smashed[4] the wooden panels[5] of the door. He swung four more times before the lock broke and the strongly built door fell backwards into the office.

Suddenly everything went quiet and the two men, shocked at the violence they had done, looked cautiously[6] into the room through the open doorway[7].

At first sight, everything seemed quite normal. The office was lit by a lamp and there was a good fire burning, with a kettle of boiling water in front of it. Nearby there were things laid out for tea. A couple of drawers were open, and there were some papers neatly[8] arranged[9] on the desk. Except for the cupboards filled with powders and chemicals it looked like any quiet, ordinary[10] office you might find anywhere in London.

But as they looked more closely, in the middle of the room there was something unusual. The body of a man lay there, face down, twitching[11] slightly. They rolled him over and recognized the face of Mr Edward Hyde. He was dressed in clothes that were too big for him, but were the right size for the doctor.

1 break down 破裂
2 mercy [ˋmɝsɪ] (n.) 慈悲；仁慈
3 swing [swɪŋ] (v.) 揮舞
4 smash [smæʃ] (v.) 粉碎；猛撞
5 panel [ˋpænl̩] (n.) 門的嵌板
6 cautiously [ˋkɔʃəslɪ] (adv.) 謹慎地
7 doorway [ˋdor͵we] (n.) 出入口；門口
8 neatly [ˋnitlɪ] (adv.) 整潔地
9 arrange [əˋrendʒ] (v.) 安排
10 ordinary [ˋɔrdn̩͵ɛrɪ] (a.) 普通的
11 twitch [twɪtʃ] (v.) 抽搐；痙攣

44 Although the body made small movements, it was only the muscles[1] and nerves[2] moving after death. Life was gone from the body. In his hand was a small glass container[3] with a distinct smell like bitter almonds[4]. Utterson knew that smell. It was the smell of arsenic[5], a fatal[6] poison[7], and Hyde had killed himself with it.

"We are too late," said Utterson, "either to save him or to punish him. Hyde has killed himself. Now we need to find Dr Jekyll's body."

They made a thorough[8] search of the office, the laboratory, the corridor[9], the large cellar[10] and the many smaller rooms in the building. There was no sign of Henry Jekyll, alive or dead, anywhere.

"Perhaps he's buried here," said Poole, stamping on the floor of the corridor, and listening to hear if it was hollow.

"Or maybe he has escaped," said Utterson, going to look at the door that led out to the side street. "But this door is still locked."

And then they found the key lying near the door, rusty[11], broken and obviously unused for a long time.

"It looks as though someone has stamped on it to break it," said Poole.

"Yes, even the broken surfaces[12] are rusty. I don't understand any of this, Poole. Let's go back to the office."

1 muscle [ˋmʌsl̩] (n.) 肌肉
2 nerve [nɝv] (n.) 神經
3 container [kənˋtenɚ] (n.) 容器
4 almond [ˋɑmənd] (n.) 杏仁
5 arsenic [ˋɑrsn̩ɪk] (n.) 砷；砒霜
6 fatal [ˋfetl̩] (a.) 致命的
7 poison [ˋpɔɪzn̩] (n.) 毒物
8 thorough [ˋθɝo] (a.) 徹底的
9 corridor [ˋkɔrɪdɚ] (n.) 走廊
10 cellar [ˋsɛlɚ] (n.) 地窖
11 rusty [ˋrʌstɪ] (a.) 生鏽的
12 surface [ˋsɝfɪs] (n.) 表面
13 heap [hip] (n.) 一堆
14 measure [ˋmɛʒɚ] (v.) 測量；估量
15 experiment [ɪkˋspɛrəmənt] (n.) 實驗
16 carry out 實踐
17 roughly [ˋrʌflɪ] (adv.) 粗糙地
18 tidy [ˋtaɪdɪ] (a.) 整潔的

They were both puzzled and worried as they went back into the office to make a thorough search. On the table they saw the chemicals the man had been working with. Small heaps[13] of white salt had been carefully measured[14] out on to small glass plates, ready for an experiment[15] that the unhappy man had been about to carry out[16].

"That is the same drug I brought to him," said Poole.

The kettle by the fire boiled over just then. They saw the armchair with a tea cup next to it, sugar already in the cup. There was one of Jekyll's favorite books there, but with angry words roughly[17] written all over the open page. They saw the large mirror, turned to face the ceiling. Then they moved to the desk. On it they saw a tidy[18] pile of papers.

46

On top of these papers there was a large envelope, with Mr Utterson's name written on it in Dr Jekyll's handwriting. The lawyer opened it and a number of smaller envelopes fell out. One was Dr Jekyll's new will, made up of[1] the same unusual paragraphs as the last, but with one important difference. In place of Mr Hyde inheriting all Dr Jekyll's property and money, Jekyll had written the name 'Gabriel John Utterson'.

Mr Utterson was amazed. He looked up at Poole, back to the will, then at the body on the floor.

"I don't believe it!" said Utterson. "Hyde had this will in his possession here. He must have been angry to see his name replaced by mine. He certainly hated me. But he did not destroy this paper."

Then he looked at the next document. It was a short note dated the same day, in Dr Jekyll's handwriting.

"Poole, the doctor was alive and here today!" said Utterson. "He cannot have been killed and the body moved in such a short time. He must still be alive. He must have run away. And if that is so, did Hyde really kill himself, or did Dr Jekyll do it? We must be careful or we will make more trouble for the doctor!"

1 be made up of 由……組成
2 confession [kən`fɛʃən] (n.) 供認；自白

"Why don't you read the note, sir?" suggested Poole.

"I am afraid to read it," said Utterson. "Though I hope I have no reason to be afraid."

He looked at the paper, and this is what he read:

> My Dear Utterson,
>
> When you read this I shall be gone. I don't know how or where, but I'm sure that the end is certain and must be soon. First, read the document Lanyon told you about, then, if you want to know more, read the confession[2] of
>
> Your unhappy friend
>
> Henry Jekyll

48 "There was a third envelope?" asked Utterson.

"Here, sir," said Poole, handing it to him.

This third envelope was a large one, carefully sealed. Mr Utterson put it in his pocket, saying to Poole, "Say nothing of this paper. We may be able to do some good for[1] your employer if he has run away, or if he is dead. It's ten o'clock now. I will go home and read these papers privately and be back here by midnight. Then we shall call the police."

The two men went out and locked the door behind them. Utterson left the servants gathered together near the fire in the hall and walked slowly and unhappily back to his office to read the two papers that would tell him the answers to what had happened.

The letters

- What do you think are in the two letters?
- Do you ever write or receive letters?
- Write a letter to a friend explaining how you feel today.

1 do good for someone 對某人做些好事
2 registered [ˋrɛdʒɪstɚd] (a.) 掛號的
3 puzzling [ˋpʌzḷɪŋ] (a.) 令人感到困惑的

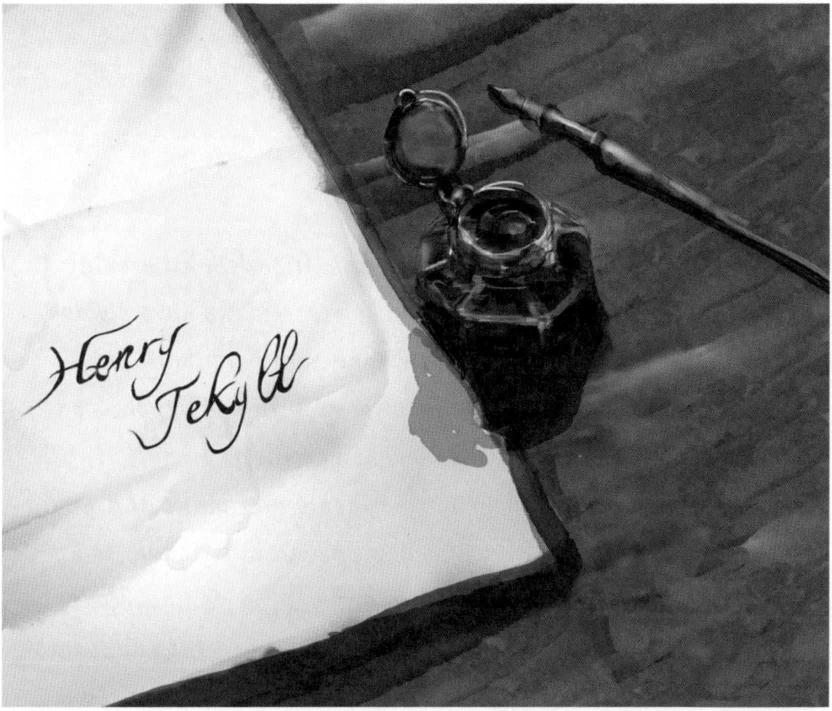

Dr Lanyon's Narrative

49 On 9th January, four days ago, I received a registered[2] letter from my old friend Henry Jekyll. I was surprised because we did not often write letters to each other. I had seen him just the previous day – in fact I had dinner with him and he did not mention any letter. I could not imagine why he had written to me, and especially why he needed to send it by registered post. What the letter said was even more puzzling[3]. It read like this:

50

Dear Lanyon,

You are one of my oldest and best friends, and even if we have disagreed about scientific matters, we have always stayed friends. I was always willing to do anything for you, and now I need your help for me. My life depends on you. If you do not help me tonight I am lost[1].

Please cancel all your appointments and plans and, taking this letter with you, call a cab and go straight to my house. Poole has his instructions and will be waiting. You are to break into[2] my office, go in alone, open the cupboard marked 'E' and take out the fourth drawer from the top with all its contents, just as they are. So that you will know you have the right drawer, I will tell you the contents. There will be some powders, a small glass container and a book. Please carry this drawer back with you to your house in Cavendish Square[3].

That's the first thing I need you to do; now for the second. If you start now, you should be back home long before midnight. Then at midnight, when no-one else is awake, a man will come to your door. He will mention my name. You must let him in yourself. Do not let your servants do this. You must then give him the drawer you brought back from my office. If you ask the man for an explanation, you will see that all of these actions are important. Otherwise I might die or become mad.

Please, please, do as I ask. If you do, all will be well. If you do not . . . well, I cannot think of the possibility. Just remember that if you do as I ask, all my troubles[4] will be over. Please do as I say and save Your friend

H. J.

PS It is possible the post office will not deliver[5] this tonight and this letter will not be in your hands until tomorrow morning. If that happens, please do as I ask whenever it is best for you during the day. The man will come again at midnight. However, by then it may already be too late, so if he does not appear at midnight, you will know you have seen the last of your friend Henry Jekyll.

1 lost [lɔst] (a.) 毀滅的
2 break into 闖入
3 square [skwɛr] (n.) 廣場
4 trouble [ˋtrʌbl̩] (n.) 麻煩；問題
5 deliver [dɪˋlɪvɚ] (v.) 投遞

51

When I read this, I thought Jekyll had gone mad. But until I knew this for certain, I felt I should do as he asked. The less I knew about what was happening, the less I could decide, and I could not ignore such a serious request. So I called a cab and drove straight to Jekyll's house.

Poole was waiting. He had also received a registered letter, with instructions to call for a locksmith[1] and carpenter[2]. It took the locksmith two hours to unlock the door without a key. The carpenter said the door was so strong he didn't think we could have broken it down.

When we got in to the office, I went to the cupboard marked 'E' and I found it unlocked. I took out the drawer, packed it with straw[3] to keep the contents in place and stop them from breaking, and then tied a cloth around the whole thing. I then returned home to Cavendish Square.

There I looked at the contents of the drawer. There were a number of salt-like powders wrapped[4] in paper. It was clear that Jekyll had prepared these because they were not in the original[5] packaging[6]. The small glass container was about half-full of a blood-red liquid. It had a very strong smell, and seemed to me to contain phosphorus[7] and some volatile[8] ether[9].

The book was an ordinary notebook and contained little except a series of dates. These covered a period of many years, but I noticed that they stopped suddenly almost a year ago. There were some short notes next to some of the dates, usually just a single word such as, "Double" which appeared perhaps six times in several hundred dates, and once very early in the list, the words "Total failure!" Although this made me very curious, it told me little that I understood.

1 locksmith [ˋlɑk͵smɪθ] (n.) 鎖匠
2 carpenter [ˋkɑrpəntɚ] (n.) 木匠
3 straw [strɔ] (n.) 稻草；麥稈
4 wrap [ræp] (v.) 包裹
5 original [əˋrɪdʒənl̩] (a.) 原來的
6 packaging [ˋpækɪdʒɪŋ] (n.) 包裝
7 phosphorus [ˋfɑsfərəs] (n.) 磷
8 volatile [ˋvɑlətl̩] (a.) 易揮發的
9 ether [ˋiθɚ] (n.) 乙醚

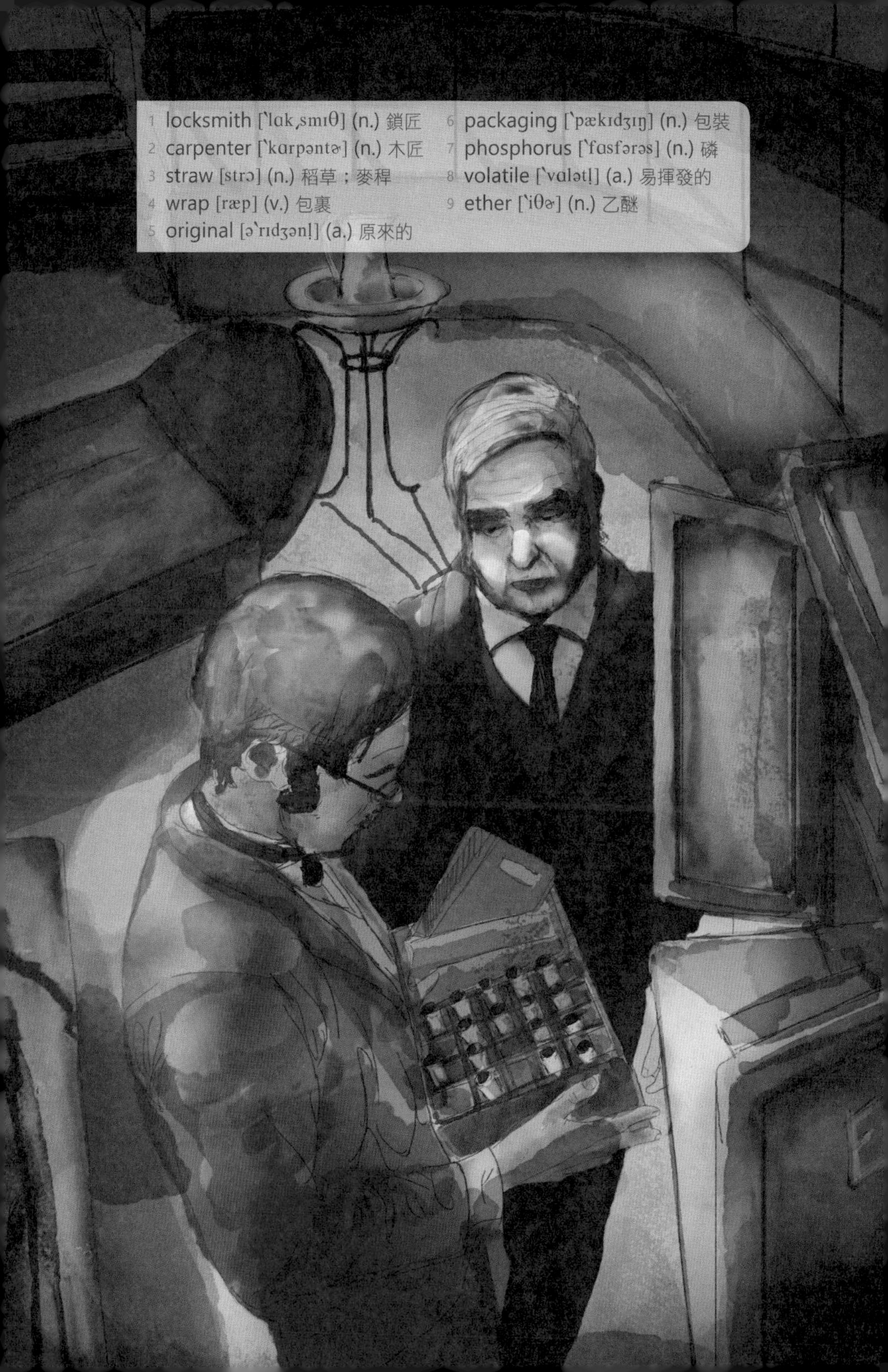

52 The glass container, the drug, and the notebook appeared to be connected with unsuccessful experiments. And that was all. How could these ordinary articles[1] be so important to the life of my friend? I did not understand.

The more I thought about it, the more I thought Jekyll had gone mad, and there might even be something dangerous about the matter. I sent my servants to bed, got out an old pistol[2] to protect myself, and waited.

Just after midnight there was a gentle knock at the door. I opened it a little. "Are you from Dr Jekyll?" I asked.

The man, a small, nervous-looking person, answered "Yes" and I invited him in.

As he came in, he looked back over his shoulder and saw a policeman at the far end of the dark street. This seemed to make him hurry inside.

I showed him into my office, all the time keeping my hand on my pistol. There in the bright light I had the chance to see him clearly. I had never seen him before; that was certain. He was small, and he had a shocking expression on his face, which looked both ill and restless[3]. I felt very uncomfortable in his company.

He was dressed in a way which would normally have made me laugh. The clothes, although of good quality, were so large that he had to roll up his trousers[4] to keep them from the ground, his collar was resting on his shoulders, and the waist of the coat was around his hips[5]. At any other time I think this would be funny, but it was not funny to me then. I was wondering where on earth[6] this strange unpleasant man came from, and what he was doing.

53

All this took just a few seconds of my thoughts. The visitor seemed very excited. "Have you got it? Have you got it?" he cried, grabbing hold[7] of my arm.

I pushed his hand away, but at the touch of his hand I could feel my blood running cold.

"Come in, sir," I said. "You forget that I have not yet the pleasure of your acquaintance[8]. Be seated, if you please." And, as an example, I sat down in my favorite chair.

"I beg your pardon[9], Dr Lanyon," he replied. "You are right. I am forgetting my manners in my haste[10]. I am here at the request of Dr Henry Jekyll, your colleague, on important business. I understand you have . . . you have . . ." He was trying hard to stay calm, but not succeeding. "I understand . . . a drawer . . .."

At this point I felt sorry for him. "There it is, sir, on the floor," I said, pointing to the drawer where it lay behind the table, still covered with the cloth.

He jumped up and ran towards it, then stopped and put his hand over his heart. I could hear his teeth grinding[11] against each other. His face was so horrible to look at, I feared for his life. He let out a loud shout of joy when he uncovered the drawer and saw the contents.

Suddenly he became quite calm. "Do you have a measuring glass[12]?" he asked.

1 article [ˋɑrtɪkl̩] (n.) 物品
2 pistol [ˋpɪstl̩] (n.) 手槍
3 restless [ˋrɛstlɪs] (a.) 焦躁不安的
4 trousers [ˋtraʊzɚz] (n.)〔複〕長褲
5 hips [hɪps] (n.)〔複〕臀部
6 on earth 究竟
7 grab hold 用手抓住
8 not yet the pleasure of your acquaintance 之前未曾謀面
9 I beg your pardon 請原諒我
10 haste [hest] (n.) 急忙
11 grind [graɪnd] (v.) 磨；碾
12 measuring glass 量杯

54

I got up from my place and gave him what he asked for. He thanked me with a smile and measured some of the red liquid into it, adding some of the powder. At this the contents began to change color as the salt diluted[1] into the liquid. It started red, then became brighter. It began to bubble[2]. Suddenly the bubbling stopped and it became dark purple, which faded[3] slowly to a watery green.

The man had watched all these changes very closely. Now he put the glass down on the table and turned to me. "Now sir, will you allow me to take this glass away and leave your house without further discussion, or is the greed[4] of curiosity too much for you? Think before you answer, because you will not be able to change your mind. Either you will be left as you are, simply having helped a fellow human being, or you will open up for yourself a terrible new area of knowledge and you will see something that your eyes will never believe."

"Sir," I said with a calmness[5] I did not feel, "you speak enigmas[6]. And you will not be surprised that I don't believe you. But I have gone too far to pause before I see the end."

"Very well. Remember your duty of secrecy as a doctor, Lanyon. What you will now see stays between us, and only us. You did not believe my scientific ideas before, so watch closely!"

With that, he put the glass to his lips and drank all the liquid from it in one gulp[7]. A cry followed, then he turned, he staggered[8], he grabbed[9] the table and held on[10], staring and gasping[11] all the time.

1 dilute [daɪˋlut] (v.) 稀釋
2 bubble [ˋbʌbl̩] (v.) 冒泡
3 fade [fed] (v.) 褪色
4 greed [grid] (n.) 貪心；貪婪
5 calmness [ˋkɑmnɪs] (n.) 平靜；鎮定
6 enigma [ɪˋnɪgmə] (n.) 難以理解的事物
7 gulp [gʌlp] (v.) 大口地飲
8 stagger [ˋstægɚ] (v.) 搖搖晃晃
9 grab [græb] (v.) 抓取
10 hold on 繼續；保持
11 gasp [gæsp] (v.) 喘氣

As I watched him, I saw a change in his appearance. He seemed to swell[1], his face suddenly became black, and the features of his face started changing shape.

"O God!" I screamed[2]. There in front of me, pale and shaking, half fainting, feeling around him with his hands like a man back from the dead, stood Henry Jekyll!

For the next hour he told me his story as I listened with horror and disbelief[3]. I still do not know if I believe it and cannot bring myself to write it down on paper. I saw what I saw, and I heard what I heard, but I don't know if I can believe my own eyes or ears. I just don't know.

Even now, I cannot sleep; fear and terror are within me all the time. I think there are only a few days of my life left, and I will die in confusion[4] and terror. I will tell you just one thing, Utterson, and that will be more than enough for you, if you can believe it. I will say that the man who entered my house that night was, according to Jekyll himself, Edward Hyde, the man known everywhere in the country as the murderer of Sir Danvers Carew.

HASTIE LANYON

Jekyll and Hyde

- The Dr Jekyll and Mr Hyde character is an example of a character with a dual personality. Other characters include:
  The Incredible Hulk
  Two Face (in the Batman series)
  Clark Kent / Superman
- Discuss these characters in pairs. How are they similar to the Jekyll / Hyde character? How are they different?

Henry Jekyll's Full Statement of the Case

56 I was born to a wealthy[5] family. As I was also physically[6] fit[7], hard-working and wanted good people to think well of me, it seemed that I had a good future ahead. My worst fault was probably that I was too eager[8] to enjoy myself like many other people before me. But I found it difficult to do this and at the same time to keep the respectable and dignified[9] reputation that I valued so much. Therefore I tried to hide my pleasures behind my other characteristics[10] of seriousness and respectability.

In time, the pleasures enjoyed by my "bad" side became worse and more shameful, which caused a lot of worry and concern to my "good" side.

When I reached a mature[11] age and thought seriously about my life and the position I had reached, I realized that there was a very deep division[12] between the respectable part of my life and the pleasure-seeking part. My two sides were very different in nature and did not fit together at all. Many men would not worry about this difference, and would even be happy to tell everyone about everything they did. I was not like that. I felt ashamed[13]. My hopes and ambitions[14] for my future were so high that I wanted to hide those parts of my character that did not entirely agree with my aims[15].

1 swell [swɛl] (v.) 腫脹
2 scream [skrim] (v.) 尖叫
3 disbelief [ˌdɪsbə`lif] (n.) 不相信
4 confusion [kən`fjuʒən] (n.) 困惑
5 wealthy [`wɛlθɪ] (a.) 富有的
6 physically [`fɪzɪklɪ] (adv.) 身體上
7 fit [fɪt] (a.) 強健的
8 eager [`igɚ] (a.) 渴望的
9 dignified [`dɪgnəˌfaɪd] (a.) 高貴的
10 characteristic [ˌkærəktə`rɪstɪk] (n.) 特色
11 mature [mə`tjur] (a.) 成熟的
12 division [də`vɪʒən] (n.) 分開
13 ashamed [ə`ʃemd] (a.) 羞愧的
14 ambition [æm`bɪʃən] (n.) 雄心；抱負
15 aim [em] (n.) 目標

57 It was therefore my ambition that was the cause of the problem rather than any particularly bad faults I had. In most men good and bad are connected. With me, they became divided from each other, and I followed both quite honestly, but separately[1].

This in turn led me to think a lot about the dual nature of man – good and bad. I worked as hard as I played, and in my scientific studies I began to think that man has not one nature, or character, but two. It is this discovery[2] that has ruined[3] my life. I say man has two characters because that is as far as my knowledge has gone. Perhaps in future other scientists will find out more than me and find that it is more than two and that man has a great range of different natures within one person.

In my own person I clearly saw two very different natures and began to wonder whether they could be separated into two separate identities[4] – two physically different people with different bodies. I began to dream of such a possibility, even before my scientific experiments showed it might be possible. If the two natures could be completely separated, the big difference between them would not worry my "good" side so much, and my life would be easier. My "bad" personality could happily go its own way and not trouble my "good" personality. But how could these natures be separated?

Personalities

- Think of your own personality. What are your good points? What are your bad points?
- What would you like to change?

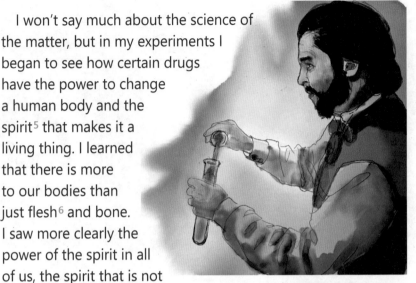

58

I won't say much about the science of the matter, but in my experiments I began to see how certain drugs have the power to change a human body and the spirit[5] that makes it a living thing. I learned that there is more to our bodies than just flesh[6] and bone. I saw more clearly the power of the spirit in all of us, the spirit that is not material[7] and which cannot therefore be caught and examined.

However, as you will hear, my experiments were never completed. It's enough to say that I was able to produce a drug that I thought would make it possible to replace the spirit and body that made up the "normal" Henry Jekyll by a second spirit and body that would be the "bad" side of me.

I hesitated before I put this theory to practice. I knew well that I risked death. I might easily lose the spirit and body of myself as Henry Jekyll completely, and never be able to become him again. But the temptation[8] of discovery was strong and I overcame[9] my fears. I bought a large quantity[10] of a particular salt, which I knew from my experiments to be the final ingredient[11] required[12].

1 separately [ˋsɛpərɪtlɪ] (adv.) 分開地
2 discovery [dɪsˋkʌvərɪ] (n.) 發現
3 ruin [ˋruɪn] (v.) 毀滅
4 identity [aɪˋdɛntətɪ] (n.) 身分
5 spirit [ˋspɪrɪt] (n.) 靈魂
6 flesh [flɛʃ] (n.) 肌肉；肉體
7 material [məˋtɪrɪəl] (a.) 物質的
8 temptation [tɛmpˋteʃən] (n.) 誘惑
9 overcome [͵ovəˋkʌm] (v.) 克服
10 quantity [ˋkwɑntətɪ] (n.) 數量
11 ingredient [ɪnˋgridɪənt] (n.) 組成成份
12 require [rɪˋkwaɪr] (v.) 需要

1 freedom [ˋfridəm] (n.) 自由
2 reflection [rɪˋflɛkʃən] (n.) 反射；映象
3 transfer [trænsˋfɝ] (v.) 轉移
4 develop [dɪˋvɛləp] (v.) 發展
5 mixture [ˋmɪkstʃɚ] (n.) 混合

59 Then late one night, I mixed the ingredients and watched them boil and smoke in the laboratory. When it was ready, I drank the liquid.

The first time I took the drug I was in great pain. My bones hurt, I felt sick and had a great horror of the spirit. Then the feeling quickly passed and I felt as though I was getting well after a serious illness. There was something new in the way I felt. It was a sweet, younger, happier feeling. I knew a kind of freedom[1]. I knew I was more wicked, and more evil, and even this thought made me happy. I also noticed I became smaller. There was no mirror in my office at that time, so I went out of the laboratory to my bedroom, and saw there in the mirror for the first time the reflection[2] of Edward Hyde.

Most of my life had been working for good as Dr Jekyll. Now I transferred[3] all the bad side of my character, which had not been as developed[4] or as strong, to this new form of Hyde. Perhaps that is why Edward Hyde was smaller, lighter and younger. His character had been used less and was therefore not as well-developed. Even his ugliness seemed natural and welcome to me as honestly showing the "bad" side of my nature. In the same way, you could say that Dr Jekyll's kindly face showed his character was mostly good. I noticed people did not want to come near me when I was Hyde. I believe all humans are a mixture[5] of good and evil, but I believe Hyde was pure evil.

I did not spend much time looking at myself as Edward Hyde in the mirror. I needed to continue to the next part of the experiment. This second part was to see if I could return to the body and person of Dr Jekyll, or whether I had lost him for ever.

60

If I had lost him, I would have to leave the house before daylight as it would no longer be my home. So I repeated the experiment, preparing and drinking the liquid. After the same suffering as before, I once again became the person and body of Henry Jekyll.

That night I had come to a fatal crossroads[1]. The drug itself was neither good nor evil – it was just a drug. At that moment it was still possible to make good use of it. I had now two characters as well as two appearances. One was wholly[2] evil, and the other was still the old Henry Jekyll, that mixture of good and bad that I was trying to reform[3].

As Henry Jekyll, I was still looking to enjoy myself in those days. But as my pleasures were not very respectable, it was not appropriate[4] to enjoy them in the respectable form of Henry Jekyll. And it seemed to me to be better to take my low pleasures in the form and person of Edward Hyde rather than in the body of the older and more respectable Dr Jekyll.

It was easy to mix the drug and in a moment, like a disguise[5], take the form of Hyde. It amused me to become Hyde. But both forms were actually me, and both felt natural. I began to arrange my life so that I could take full advantage[6] of the situation.

The transformation

- Why does Jekyll choose to become Hyde? Tick the best answer.
  - ☐ Because he wants to continue with his scientific research.
  - ☐ Because he wants to stop being respectable.
  - ☐ Because he wants to use Hyde for his pleasure-seeking activities.

61

I bought a house in Soho for Hyde to live in, and employed a quiet and not very respectable woman who would not ask too many questions. I told my servants that Hyde was to have free use of my house and property, and occasionally[7] I became Hyde and visited Jekyll's house so that they would become used to the idea. I even made the will in Hyde's favor. This was the will that you, Utterson, did not like. But I needed to do it so that if anything happened to Jekyll I could continue my life of evil pleasure as Mr Hyde.

In this way I could therefore lead my two different lives of respectability on the one hand and pleasure on the other. I could lead the two lives quite separately and safe in the knowledge[8] I would keep my money and property whatever[9] happened.

I felt completely safe. I was free to do whatever evil I wanted as Edward Hyde, but in a moment I could become the completely respectable Henry Jekyll! No-one could catch me. I could not be held responsible at all.

My pleasures were not respectable, but they became even more terrible in the hands of Mr Hyde. Sometimes Henry Jekyll was shocked by Hyde's actions, but he didn't feel responsible for them. Hyde was not him. Jekyll still had his good qualities and even, when possible, tried to undo the evil that Hyde did. But still he did not feel responsible.

1 crossroads [ˋkrɔs,rodz] (n.) 十字路口
2 wholly [ˋholɪ] (adv.) 完全地
3 reform [rɪˋfɔrm] (v.) 改造
4 appropriate [əˋproprɪ,et] (a.) 適當的
5 disguise [dɪsˋgaɪz] (n.) 偽裝；掩飾
6 advantage [ədˋvæntɪdʒ] (n.) 優勢
7 occasionally [əˋkeʒənḷɪ] (adv.) 偶而
8 in the knowledge 在知道……的情況下
9 whatever [hwɑtˋɛvɚ] (pron.) 不管什麼

62

When I started on this path[1], I did not see what would happen in the end. I had no idea that it would. I did however have some warning of how things would turn out. I can give you one example of this, although nothing very bad happened to me as a result of[2] it.

I accidentally knocked over a young girl in the street and this made me so angry that I kicked her. This made a passer-by[3] angry. I recognized him the other day as your cousin. The child's family and a doctor joined him and for a while I feared for my life. They were all so angry, and the women were so threatening[4], that I thought it was best to pay them money to make them go away quietly.

I was Edward Hyde, but I had to bring them to Jekyll's laboratory door and pay them with a check in Henry Jekyll's name. This must have seemed very strange to them. After this I made sure to open another bank account in Edward Hyde's name, so this kind of situation need not happen again.

Then, about two months before the murder of Sir Danvers Carew, I came home late after one of my night-time adventures[5] and went to sleep, as Jekyll, in Jekyll's house. After I woke up late in the morning, I slowly began to feel something was not normal. But as I was so sleepy I did not worry too much about it and dozed[6] off back to sleep.

After a while I woke again and happened to see my hand on the bed sheet. To my shock, it was not the large, firm[7] hand of Henry Jekyll, but the thin, dark and hairy one of Edward Hyde.

1 path [pæθ] (n.) 小徑；途徑
2 as a result of 由於
3 passer-by [ˋpæsɚˋbaɪ] (n.) 過路人
4 threatening [ˋθrɛtṇɪŋ] (a.) 脅迫的
5 adventure [ədˋvɛntʃɚ] (n.) 冒險
6 doze [doz] (v.) 打瞌睡
7 firm [fɝm] (a.) 結實的

63

I jumped out of bed in horror and rushed to the mirror. It chilled[1] my blood to see Edward Hyde looking back at me from the mirror! I had gone to bed as Henry Jekyll and I had woken up as Edward Hyde. How had this happened? And how could it be corrected[2]?

I was very frightened. I needed to get to the laboratory, but how was I to get there through the house at this time of the morning without the servants seeing me? My drugs were all in the office, a long journey[3], down two flights of stairs, along a corridor, across the courtyard and through the laboratory. I could cover my face, perhaps, but what about my size?

Then suddenly I realized that this was not a problem after all. The servants already knew me as Hyde, though they had not seen me at this time of day. So I got dressed as well as I could in Jekyll's clothes and went through the house. The servants stared[4] when they saw me at such an hour and in such strange clothes, but ten minutes later Dr Jekyll had returned to his own appearance and was sitting down with his breakfast as usual.

As you can imagine, my appetite[5] was small. This inexplicable[6] incident[7] made me reflect[8] more seriously on the issues[9] and possibilities of my double existence[10]. Hyde was becoming a more powerful character, and I began to sense the danger that if this continued, the character of Edward Hyde could gain control[11].

I already had to take larger amounts of the drug in order to stop being Hyde, whereas in the beginning the difficulty had been to change from Jekyll into Hyde. I was slowly losing hold of[12] my original and better self and I was becoming my second and worse self.

1 chill [tʃɪl] (v.) 使感到寒冷
2 correct [kəˋrɛkt] (v.) 改正
3 journey [ˋdʒɝnɪ] (v.) 旅行
4 stare [stɛr] (v.) 盯；凝視
5 appetite [ˋæpə͵taɪt] (n.) 食慾；胃口
6 inexplicable [ɪnˋɛksplɪkəbl̩] (a.) 無法說明的

64

I now felt I had to decide between these two. But how could I make this decision? The only thing they had in common was a shared memory. Everything else about them was different.

Jekyll was actually a mix of the two sides. He shared Hyde's adventures and sometimes enjoyed them, even though he did not always approve[13] of them. Hyde, by contrast[14], had no interest in, and just a faint[15] memory of, Jekyll's life. Jekyll had an interest in Hyde, in the same way that a father is interested in a son. But Hyde had less interest in Jekyll's life than any son has in his father's.

To become Jekyll would mean to lose all the pleasures that I enjoyed; to become Hyde would mean to lose a thousand interests and ambitions, as well as all his friends. It seemed an easy choice to make. I would lose more as Hyde than I would as Jekyll. However, it was not that simple. Whereas Jekyll would feel the loss of pleasure, Hyde would not even be conscious[16] of all that he had lost.

The choice

- Why would he choose to stay as Hyde? Why would he choose to stay as Jekyll?
- Have you ever had to make a difficult choice? What was it? How did you reach your decision?

7 incident [ˋɪnsədn̩t] (n.) 事件
8 reflect [rɪˋflɛkt] (v.) 思考；反省
9 issue [ˋɪʃjʊ] (n.) 問題
10 existence [ɪgˋzɪstəns] (n.) 存在
11 gain control 取得控制權
12 lose hold of 失去對……的掌握
13 approve [əˋpruv] (v.) 贊成；同意
14 by contrast 相形之下
15 faint [fent] (a.) 模糊的
16 conscious [ˋkɑnʃəs] (a.) 意識到的

65 Well, like many men before me, although these were very different circumstances[1] from any that came before, I decided to choose to stay as my better side, Dr Jekyll. For two whole months I was Dr Jekyll, and only Dr Jekyll. But I was lacking in strength to keep to my promise. Perhaps the fact that I had kept Hyde's clothes in my office and did not sell Hyde's house showed that I wasn't ready to give him up[2] for ever. But for two whole months I kept strictly[3] to my decision. I led a pure life and worked hard.

However, time began to remove the terrible memories that Hyde's life had left me and I began to thirst[4] for his pleasures again. At last, in a weak moment, I prepared and swallowed[5] the drug once again. But I was not prepared for the complete lack of morals[6] or readiness to[7] evil that were evident in Hyde. My devil had been locked away for two months and he came out roaring[8] and more evil than before.

When the drug took effect[9] I immediately went wild and attacked a man who approached me politely in the street. My victim[10] was struck down without warning and without any human feelings. I was cold and ruthless[11]. I enjoyed every blow, and continued hitting my victim until he was lying dead and lifeless on the ground. Still I continued, full of anger, and only stopped when I was too tired to continue. Then suddenly I realized my life was in danger and I ran from the scene of these excesses[12]. I went back to Hyde's house in Soho where I destroyed my papers. I then set out for Jekyll's house, thinking over what I had done and planning similar attacks for the future.

1 circumstances [ˋsɝkəm͵stænsɪs] (n.)〔複〕情況
2 give up 放棄
3 strictly [ˋstrɪktlɪ] (adv.) 嚴格地
4 thirst [θɝst] (v.) 渴望
5 swallow [ˋswɑlo] (v.) 吞
6 morals [ˋmɔrəlz] (n.)〔複〕道德
7 readiness to 願意……
8 roar [ror] (v.) 咆哮
9 take effect 生效
10 victim [ˋvɪktɪm] (n.) 受害者
11 ruthless [ˋruθlɪs] (a.) 無情的
12 excess [ɪkˋsɛs] (n.) 暴行

66

When I became Jekyll again, Hyde's joy changed to tears of regret[1] and sorrow. I saw my life pass before my eyes. All I had worked for, and all I had achieved[2], ended in this terrible evening. I realized I must not become Hyde again, whether[3] I wanted to or not. I could only live if I stayed as Jekyll, my better part. How grateful I was at this thought! I locked the door Hyde used and destroyed the key. He could never gain access[4] again.

The next day I heard the news of the murder. I heard that the victim was a well-liked[5] man and that Hyde was known to be the murderer. This was enough reason for me never to become Hyde again, and to understand that the killing was a foolish act. If I became Hyde again, it would mean death for me.

So from that time forward I decided to live a life of good deeds[6]. I enjoyed this blameless[7] life, but sometimes my dual nature still gave me problems. I did not want to live as Hyde again, even the idea of that alarmed[8] me. But I could feel from time to time my dark side growling[9] beneath the surface.

One fine January day I was sitting in the sun in Regent's Park. The animal within me was dreaming of the past, while the spiritual side promised that I would forget these thoughts immediately. At that very moment a horrible nausea[10] came over me. I began to feel a change in my thoughts and feelings. I looked down: my clothes hung on my shrunken[11] body and the hand on my knee was rough[12] and hairy. I was once more Edward Hyde, the man the whole of London was hunting as a murderer!

1 regret [rɪ`grɛt] (v.) 後悔
2 achieve [ə`tʃiv] (v.) 實現；完成
3 whether [`hwɛðɚ] (conj.) 是否
4 access [`æksɛs] (n.) 進入
5 well-liked [`wɛl`laɪkt] (a.) 受歡迎的
6 deed [did] (n.) 行為
7 blameless [`blemlɪs] (a.) 無過失的
8 alarm [ə`lɑrm] (v.) 使恐懼
9 growl [graʊl] (v.) 嗥叫；咆哮
10 nausea [`nɔʃɪə] (n.) 極端的憎惡
11 shrink [ʃrɪŋk] (v.) 縮小
12 rough [rʌf] (a.) 粗糙的

I could only change back to Henry Jekyll with the help of the drug, but how was I to get it without being caught[1]? My mind focused sharply on this problem in a way I had noticed before when I became Edward Hyde. Jekyll might have given up, but Hyde was alert[2] enough to find a solution[3].

My drug was in one of the drawers in a cupboard in Jekyll's office. How could I get there? I set myself to solve this problem. I could not enter the laboratory through the back door because I had locked it and destroyed the key. If I went in through the front door, the servants would see me, catch me and give me to the police. I knew that I needed someone else to get the drug for me, and my thoughts[4] turned to Dr Lanyon. He could go to my house and get the drug from my office.

How could I ask him to do this for me? I knew he did not like Hyde. How could I ask a respectable man to break into the office of his friend – in other words to act like a thief? And if he was willing to do that, how could I then go to meet him at his house? How could I reach his house without being caught?

Then I remembered that I could still write like Dr Jekyll. I could write a note to Lanyon in Jekyll's handwriting. He knew his friend's handwriting and he would know it came from Jekyll. Once I realized that, the rest of the plan came to me very easily.

I dressed as best I could and covered as much of my face as I could, then I stopped a cab in the street. I told the driver to go to a hotel I knew about. The driver laughed at my ill-fitting[5] clothes, but soon stopped when he saw my anger. It was lucky for him that he stopped! I could easily have done him a lot of harm if he had continued. I wanted to hurt him.

1 catch [kætʃ] (v.) 逮捕
2 alert [əˋlɝt] (a.) 警覺的
3 solution [səˋluʃən] (n.) 解決辦法
4 thought [θɔt] (n.) 想法
5 ill-fitting [ˋɪlˋfɪtɪŋ] (a.) 不合的

68 At the hotel, the staff[1] took me to a private room. Seeing my anger, they stayed well away from me[2] after that except[3] to bring the pen and paper I demanded. As Hyde I was very angry. I wanted to hurt people. I wanted to kill. This extreme[4] feeling was new to me.

Only just managing to[5] control his anger, Hyde wrote two letters, one to Lanyon and one to Poole, and sent them off[6] by registered post.

Hyde (I cannot say 'I') waited impatiently[7] all day in his private room at the hotel, frightening the staff with his behavior and appearance. Then when it was completely dark, he took a cab and drove to and fro[8] around the city. He was full of fear and hatred. When he thought the driver had begun to grow suspicious[9] he got out and walked among the night-time pedestrians[10].

He was a strange, frightening figure in his ill-fitting clothes, walking fast and talking to himself, counting the minutes until midnight. Once a girl tried to speak to him. I think she was selling boxes of matches. He hit her in the face and she ran away.

When I came back to myself at Dr Lanyon's house, the horror on the doctor's face upset me. But it was nothing compared[11] to my horror and fear of being Hyde. I was no longer afraid of the police. I was afraid of remaining[12] Edward Hyde.

After I had done my business with Lanyon, I went home as Dr Jekyll. I hardly knew what I was doing. It was like a dream. But I was grateful for my escape and felt safe at home again. I went to bed and fell fast asleep[13] for the whole of the rest of the night.

1 staff [stæf] (n.)〔總稱〕工作人員
2 stay away from me 離得我遠遠地
3 except [ɪk`sɛpt] (prep.) 除……外
4 extreme [ɪk`strim] (a.) 極端的
5 manage to 設法
6 send off 寄出
7 impatiently [ɪm`peʃəntlɪ] (adv.) 沒耐性地
8 to and fro 往復地；來回地
9 suspicious [sə`spɪʃəs] (a.) 猜疑的
10 pedestrian [pə`dɛstrɪən] (n.) 行人
11 compare [kəm`pɛr] (v.) 比較
12 remaining [rɪ`menɪŋ] (a.) 留下的
13 fall asleep 睡著

69

I woke in the morning weak but refreshed[1]. I had not forgotten the horror of the previous[2] day, but I was home again and near my drugs. However, after breakfast I was walking across the courtyard when I began to feel that terrible change come over me again. I managed to reach the laboratory and my drug, but I had to take double the amount of the drug to change me back to being Jekyll. From that day onwards, it was only by taking large amounts of the drug and making very great efforts[3] to stay as Jekyll that I could keep Hyde away[4].

If I slept, I always woke up as Hyde. Therefore I slept as little as possible. This affected my health and I became weak and eaten by fear[5]. As Jekyll became weaker, Hyde seemed to grow stronger. Now Jekyll hated Hyde as much as Hyde hated Jekyll.

No-one has ever suffered as I have suffered. This punishment might have continued for years if this final terrible event had not happened. Now I was separated from my true nature. I could no longer be the Dr Jekyll who was once respected in the city. My supplies of the powder that made up the drug were becoming low, so I sent for[6] more. Poole tried every chemist I knew in the city, but we could not find any powder of the same quality. At first I thought that we could not find any powder which was as pure as my original powder. Now I realize that the original powder was probably not pure, and that it was this impurity[7] that made the drug work so well.

1 refreshed [rɪˋfrɛʃt] (a.) 精神恢復的
2 previous [ˋpriviəs] (a.) 先前的
3 effort [ˋɛfɚt] (n.) 努力
4 keep somebody away 使某人離開
5 be eaten by fear 被恐懼所吞噬
6 send for 派人去……
7 impurity [ɪmˋpjʊrətɪ] (n.) 雜質

70 A week has passed and I am finishing this letter just at the same time as I am finishing the last of my powder. This is the last time Henry Jekyll will be able to think his own thoughts or see his own face. If I change into Hyde while I am writing, I am sure Hyde will destroy this letter. Therefore I must finish it soon and put it in a place where he will not see it.

I know that in half an hour I will be Edward Hyde sitting here shaking and crying. How will he die? Will it be in a prison, or will he kill himself? I do not know, and I do not care. What is happening to me now is my real death, and what follows will be Hyde's death, not mine. I will now put down my pen and bring the life of that unhappy Henry Jekyll to an end.

AFTER READING

A Personal Response

1. What had you heard about Jekyll & Hyde before you read this story?

2. Is the story different from what you expected? If so, how is it different?

3. Do you think the story ends in a good way? Can you suggest why the author ends it like this?

4. Discuss other ways in which the story could have ended.

5. What three adjectives best describe this story? Explain your choices.

B Comprehension

6 Tick (✓) T (true), F (false) or D (doesn't say) below.

- T F D (a) Dr Jekyll was dead at the beginning of the book.
- T F D (b) Utterson had been a lawyer for forty years.
- T F D (c) Poole worked for Mr Utterson.
- T F D (d) Sir Danvers Carew was a client of Mr Utterson.
- T F D (e) The story takes place in London in winter.
- T F D (f) Dr Jekyll lived and worked in the same house.
- T F D (g) Utterson was worried about Dr Jekyll.
- T F D (h) Utterson approved of Dr Jekyll's will.
- T F D (i) Jekyll was younger than Utterson.
- T F D (j) Lanyon and Jekyll had studied together at university.

7 Work in pairs. Person A is a reporter for a newspaper. Person B is the servant who saw the murder of Sir Danvers Carew. The reporter must interview the servant and together A and B write the report for the newspaper.

A *At what time did you see the two men?*

B *It was about 11 o'clock at night.*

8 Discuss the following questions with a partner.

(a) What types of documents are referred to in the story? How are they important to the story?

(b) Why does Jekyll start seeing his friends again after the murder of Sir Danvers Carew?

(c) Why does Lanyon stop all contact with Dr Jekyll? What does he see that shocks him?

(d) What do Poole and Utterson expect to find when they break the door of Jekyll's laboratory?

(e) What does Dr Jekyll say about his youth in his letter to Utterson?

9 Reread the parts of the story that describe Dr Jekyll's house. Draw a plan of it, including the courtyard, laboratory, and the side street.

Dr Jekyll' House

10 "Dr Jekyll creates Mr Hyde in order to hide his own evil inclinations and continue to live a respectable life." Write a paragraph to support this statement, using examples from the book.

C Characters

11 Hyde is never fully described. What picture do you have in your mind of his appearance? Try to draw him. Why does Stevenson choose not to describe him fully?

12 Everyone who sees Hyde comments on how his presence makes them feel uncomfortable. What does Hyde symbolize? Why does this make people feel uncomfortable?

13 Hyde cannot control his anger. Find examples of this in the story. Then in groups discuss how the inability to control anger can cause serious problems. Find examples from other books, films, songs or real life (news stories).

14 Imagine you are Inspector Newcomen and you want to arrest Hyde for the murder of Sir Danvers Carew. Find as much information on Hyde as you can from the story. Then write a report to distribute to the public asking for information on Hyde and where he is.

15 Form groups of four or five. Take turns to choose a character from the book. The others ask "Yes/ No" questions in order to find out who you are.

16 In groups brainstorm words and phrases to describe the two main characters of the story, Dr Jekyll and Mr Hyde. Fill in below.

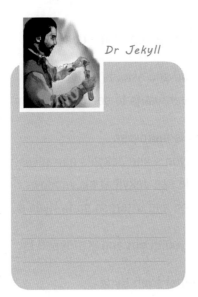

Dr Jekyll

Mr Hyde

17 In pairs imagine a conversation between Dr Jekyll and Mr Hyde. What questions would they ask each other? Act out the dialogue.

18 Choose three adjectives below to describe Utterson. Give reasons for your choices giving examples from the story.

Serious	Kind	Determined
Revengeful	Angry	Friendly
Talkative	Loyal	Patient

19 Imagine you are Utterson. Write a letter to Dr Jekyll saying you are worried about him. Ask him what is happening and offer help and advice.

D Plot and Theme

20 Put these events from the story in the correct order.

____ (a) Poole and Utterson break down the door to Jekyll's laboratory.

____ (b) Utterson meets Hyde and asks to see his face.

____ (c) Lanyon says he never wants to see or hear from Jekyll again.

____ (d) Sir Danvers Carew is murdered.

____ (e) Utterson reads Lanyon's and Jekyll's narratives.

____ (f) Utterson and Enfield see Jekyll at his window.

____ (g) Inspector Newcomen and Utterson go to Hyde's house.

____ (h) Hyde runs into the young girl and is stopped by Enfield.

____ (i) Jekyll receives a letter from Hyde.

____ (j) Enfield tells Utterson the story of the door.

____ (k) Utterson and Poole find Hyde dead in Jekyll's laboratory.

21 "Mr Hyde is the evil part that lives in all us." Divide the class into two groups and debate this statement, one side debating for the statement and one against.

22 Think of 3 questions you would ask Dr Jekyll and 3 questions you would ask Mr Hyde.

23 Letters and notes play an important part in this story. List five different letters or notes from the story and complete this table with information about them.

From	To	About

24 There were no telephones at the time of the story. Would a telephone call or text message have been better than any of the letters or notes above? Explain your answer. Write a text message from Utterson to Jekyll asking for an explanation.

25 At what stage in the story are we told that Dr Jekyll and Mr Hyde are parts of the same person?

26 Here are three possible themes to the story.

- **A** *The duality of human nature*
- **B** *The battle of good against evil*
- **C** *The importance of reputation*

Find examples in the story of each of these. Share with a partner.

TEST

1 Make connections between the characters in Column A and those in Column B. Say if they met, or if they didn't meet. Describe the connection between them. Try to use all of the characters.

Column A	Column B
Mr Utterson	Mr Enfield
Mr Lanyon	Dr Jekyll
Hyde's housekeeper	Sir Danvers Carew
Inspector Newcomen	Poole
Mr Hyde	Mr Guest

2 How does Dr Jekyll's attitude towards his dual personality change throughout the story? Write an explanation. Think of the following key moments:

1. When he was a young man
2. When he starts experiments into the human body
3. When he takes the drug for the first time
4. When Hyde knocks over the girl in the street
5. After the murder of Sir Danvers Carew
6. When he was sitting in Regent's Park
7. When he becomes Jekyll once more in Dr Lanyon's house
8. When he decides to kill himself

3 Read the following and tick (✓) the most suitable phrase to finish the sentences.

a) Poole asked Utterson to come to Jekyll's house because:

1) he couldn't open Dr Jekyll's office door.
2) he didn't know where Dr Jekyll had gone.
3) he thought someone had murdered Dr Jekyll.
4) he thought there was a burglar in Dr Jekyll's office.

b) Dr Jekyll had problems reproducing the effect of his drug because:

1) Poole couldn't find enough supplies in London.
2) he didn't realize the original ingredients were impure.
3) the chemists didn't want to help him because the drug was illegal.
4) he became immune to the drug and needed greater quantities.

c) Dr Lanyon stopped all contact with Dr Jekyll because:

1) he was jealous of the success of Jekyll's experiments.
2) he was shocked when he realized that Hyde was a part of Jekyll.
3) he disapproved of Jekyll's will.
4) he had an argument with Jekyll about scientific beliefs.

d) Poole and Utterson thought that Hyde had killed himself because:

1) he was unhappy.
2) he had already killed Dr Jekyll.
3) Jekyll could not replicate the drug.
4) he had murdered Sir Danvers Carew.

4 Join the sentences below using one of the relative pronouns in the box below.

which   who   which   who   which   whose

a) The noise had attracted a small crowd of people. The people were very angry with the man.

____

b) The check was signed by a man. I cannot tell you his name.

____

c) He went across the back garden to the building at the back. Jekyll had made the building into a laboratory.

____

d) He was small, and he had a shocking expression on his face. His face looked both ill and restless.

____

e) I think your employer could have a very painful illness. This illness also affects his appearance.

____

f) I went wild and attacked a man. The man had approached me politely in the street.

____

71 Now listen and check your answers.

5 Read the sentences in Exercise 4 once more. With a partner name the person referred to in the green underlines. Together decide when each episode occurs in the book. Check with another pair.

TRANSLATION

作者簡介

本書作者羅伯特・路易斯・史帝文生於 1850 年出生在蘇格蘭，父親為一位知名的工程師，而他本人則先後研習工程及法律。 1876 年，他成為一位專職的作者和作家，並在 1880 年娶了芬妮・歐斯朋。

史帝文生以創作遊記聞名，像是《騎驢漫遊記》（1879 年），和諸如《金銀島》（1883 年）之類的冒險故事等。史帝文生很不喜歡他在十九世紀的英國社會所看到的偽善，對二十一世紀的讀者來說，他的態度和見解算是很具現代風格。

史帝文生為疾病所苦，他與芬妮四處旅遊，以尋找對他身體健康有益的氣候條件，而旅遊也往往會為他帶來寫作的素材。

1886 到 1887 年，他和芬妮住在波恩茅斯鎮，《化身博士》和《綁架》就是在這段期間所寫成的。該小鎮位於英格蘭南岸，由於氣候宜人，所以之前就有人向他推薦這個地方，更何況他的父親還曾在這裡為他小倆口買了一間房子，做為結婚禮物。

1887 年之後，為了尋找更冒險的人生和更有益於健康的氣候，史帝文生就偕同芬妮遊遍歐洲，接著又前往太平洋。 1889 年，他們在太平洋一個叫做薩摩亞的小島上建屋居住，一直到 1894 年在那裡與世長辭。

只要屬於英語系的地區，史帝文生都一直是深受歡迎的作家，甚至還被許多法國人所追憶，而他的那本《騎驢漫遊記》，更曾幫助該地區觀光業的再興。

本書簡介

《化身博士》可能是史帝文生最有名的代表作，而「傑寇與海德」（Jekyll and Hyde）一語則成為英語中一個十分常見的用法（比如說「他同時兼具傑寇與海德的人格」），並且廣為人知，即使沒讀過本書的人也知之甚詳。

本書的主題講的是人性當中的「人格分裂」，或說是「雙重性格」。其核心概念認為，我們每一個人都會同時呈現善與惡兩種面貌，並探討如果這些部分在人體化學構造上到最後分成兩種單獨的人格的話，那究竟會發生什麼樣的事。這個主題對史帝文生來說特別親切，他以此創作了一齣劇本和一則短篇故事。

這篇故事也談到了名譽的重要性，原本備受尊敬的傑寇博士之所以開始變身為邪惡的海德先生，就是因為他害怕自己的行為失當，想挽回自己的聲譽。至於他的朋友亞特森、藍彥和安費等，也會不計一切代價的避免流言蜚語上身。維多利亞時代中對儀表和外觀的重視，也反應出名譽的重要性，而表象又是如何頻頻掩蓋了齷齪和暴力的事實。

這篇故事的架構亦饒富趣味，除了由作者所訴說的敘述外，還有兩則由主人翁針對同樣事件所撰寫的描述。對於同一事件我們算是讀了三次，但各有觀點。

這篇故事曾被譯為多種語言，而且也給無數電影、音樂劇、戲劇、故事、卡通影片和電玩遊戲等，帶來不少靈感。

一扇門的故事

P. 13

亞特森先生是位律師，他是一個有著矛盾性格的男人。他不苟言笑，所以一付拒人於千里之外的樣子，可是一旦在宴會上有朋友相伴時，就會變得很有社交手腕，和人們相處融洽；他不允許自己有奢華的享受，不會花費太多錢在自己身上；儘管他喜歡喝上好的葡萄酒，卻不會獨自飲酌；他喜歡上戲院，卻已經二十年未曾踏進劇院去看戲。然而，他樂於看到別人享受人生，不會動輒抱怨或是批評別人的生活縱情逸樂。正因為他是這樣的人，所以對那些在社會上聲譽日漸不佳、自甘墮落的人來說，亞特森律師往往是他們碩果僅存的高尚朋友。

他可以稱得上謙謙君子，因為他對朋友宅心仁厚，卻不指望別人以他為師。他能夠接受別人的真正的樣子，容納別人的缺點等等一切。和他有交往的人，大都是家族的遠親，或是多年熟識的老友。你可以這麼說，他不會主動去選擇交朋友，而是朋友們後來慢慢靠著他圍攏過來，就像長春藤依往大樹依附過來一樣。

P. 14

尤其理查·安費先生更是這樣一位朋友，他是一位遠親，在倫敦市裡大名也是響叮噹的。他們是兩個截然不同的人，但一到了星期天，都會相伴步行，走上一段長長的時間。

見過他們並肩而行的人都說，他們一路上很少開口，看起來鬱鬱寡歡的，彷彿很樂意能在路上巧遇其他友人。不過事實上，兩人是很期盼這一星期一次的散步，而且會為了出門好好散步一番，把其他的約會取消，不想被打擾。

朋友

- 你最親密的朋友有哪些？你都喜歡和他們在一起做什麼？
- 你喜歡和不同的朋友做不同的事嗎？

這天，兩人又在街上相偕而行。那是倫敦一處車水馬龍的地區，他們在一條安靜的小街道上信步而行。因為適逢星期天，這條街道很安靜，是大多數的商家都拉下了大門。要是換作平日，這裡的店家生意興隆，整條街上好不熱鬧。這條街令人感到愉悅，街道上色彩繽紛，住在這裡的居民和店家把這條街維護得很整潔美觀。更確切地說，除了那

幢兩層樓高的建築之外，整條街看起來都很整潔美觀。那幢建築位在一個開闊的走道旁，順著走道便會走出這條街。

P. 15

那幢建築在面對著街道的這一面牆上，看不到半個窗戶，光禿禿的整堵高牆只有一樓開了一扇門，顯得很不友善。牆面已經斑駁剝落，已經掉漆的大門顯得斑痕累累而污穢。門鈴和門環付之闕如，看起來像是已經廢棄的房子，小孩子在上面亂塗亂刮的那些鬼畫符，一直都未見有人清理或修復。

當兩人走過那幢建築時，安費先生問亞特森律師，是否有注意到那扇門，因為那讓安費想起了一件怪異的事情。

「我沒注意到，怎麼啦？是什麼事情？」亞特森問。

安費先生答道：「是這樣的，有一次，在一個漆黑的冬天夜裡，我在凌晨三點的時候沿著這條街走回家，整條街萬籟俱寂，猶如空城。因為實在太安靜了，我當時心想，『這時候要是有警察在，就不會那麼嚇人了』。說時遲那時快，我突然看到兩個人出現在眼前，其中一個是男人，他個子很小，長相猥瑣，快步在街上走著；另一個是年約八、九歲的小女孩，從另一條街往這條街直奔過來，結果兩人在街角處撞了個滿懷。不過不尋常的是，那個矮小的男人沒有停下來道歉，反而趁著小女孩跌落在地上時，故意用力踩過她的身體，小女孩的痛得哀叫。之後他繼續往前走，把小女孩丟在一旁。」

P. 16

「這種事真是慘不忍睹，那個男人根本不是人，他是一個機器，威力強大，無法制止。我見狀立刻大聲叫喊，並一路追著那可惡的傢伙，等到逮到他後，要把他押回他剛才撞倒小女孩的地點。

「嘈雜聲吸引了一小群人過來圍觀，包括小女孩的家人。對於那個男人的行徑，小女孩的家人義憤填膺。一個醫生來到達現場，檢查那位可憐的小女孩，她的傷勢並不嚴重，但是受到了很大的驚嚇。那個男人什麼話也沒說，也沒有逃走的企圖，他的表情非常醜陋猥瑣，令我不寒而慄。他沒有開口道歉，對於所發生的事也沒有一絲難過的神情。

P.17

「我看到醫生對他也充滿了嫌惡。眾人都出言警告他，他要是不為自己的行為付出代價，我們就要讓他好看。在這過程中，我們還得從頭到尾把他和那些想修理他的激憤婦女們隔開。

「氣憤的群眾越聚越多，大家都不肯放過他，他只好同意付給小女孩的家人一百元英鎊，以做為賠償。他顯然很不喜歡這種和解，我們擔心他會藉機逃走，不付半毛錢。

P.18

「又因為他身上沒帶那麼多錢，就說他要回家拿支票。你想，他回到了哪裡？他走進了我們眼前這幢房子的大門裡！然後拿著十鎊金幣和用來補足差額的一張支票走出來。至於支票上所簽的姓名是誰，我不能告訴你，但那個人大有來頭，名聲很好，甚至常常見報！

「我一點也不相信那個傢伙，我就這麼跟他說。有誰可以在凌晨四點鐘大剌剌地進出這麼一道門，而且過一會兒出來後，還帶著另一個人所簽的支票，面額還將近一百英鎊？這簡直是天方夜譚！因此，我們要他和那位醫生及小女孩的父親一起待在我家，等到早上銀行開門為止。後來天亮了，我們用過早餐後便殺到銀行去兌換支票。當時是我親手把支票交給櫃枱的，我心想那張支票一定是唬人的，可是讓我跌破眼鏡的是，那張支票是真的！」

亞特森先生聽到他這麼說，不禁冷哼了一聲。

信任

- 什麼是信任？請寫下定義！
- 想想看，你曾在什麼事情上信任別人？想想看，你曾在什麼事情上不信任別人？和夥伴分享你的經驗。

P.19

「我明白，你的感覺和我一樣。」安費先生說：「沒錯，這件事很令人惡厭，沒有哪個仁人君子會想跟那種人打交道，不過在支票上簽名的，卻是一個有頭有臉的名人，在社會上還做了不少善事。或許這位誠實的紳士是因為年輕時做過什麼糊塗事而被抓到把柄，所以才任由那個混蛋勒索吧！不過事情還是充滿疑團。」

「你想一個有頭有臉的人會住在這麼一棟破房子裡嗎？」一臉訝異的亞特森問道。

「不會，我有看到支票上的地址，他住在別區。讓我百思不解是，這兩個八竿子都打不到一塊兒的人怎麼會有關連？」

「你跟別人詢問過這件事嗎？」

「沒有，我不想把事情鬧大，『不惹是生非』是我的處世原則。」安費先生說。

「沒錯，你說得很對，我同意你的看法！」律師說道。

別招惹睡得正酣的狗

- 這句話是什麼意思？分成小組討論。
- 在你的母語中是否也有類似的用法？

P. 20

「這幢房子很詭異。」安費繼續說：「自從那晚起，我就在仔細研究，房子沒有其他的門，而且除了撞倒小女孩的那個混蛋偶而會現身之外，就沒有人會從這道門進出。那條通道通往中庭，二樓有三扇窗戶面向中庭，但一樓完全沒有窗戶。我看一定有人住在那兒，因為那些窗戶雖然都關得緊緊，卻很乾淨，而且裡面的煙囪也常常會有煙冒出。」

「安費啊，你剛才說的『少惹是生非』是很好的處世原則，不過我想問一下，撞倒小女孩的男人叫什麼名字？」

「我想說出來也不會怎麼樣，那個混蛋傢伙叫做海德！」安費先生答道。

「他長的什麼樣子？」

「他的樣子不是很好形容，總覺得有什麼地方不對勁，他的外表不討人喜歡，但又說不上來到底是哪裡不對勁。我沒見過像他這樣惹人厭的人，但又說不出所以然，反正整個人看起來就是怪怪的。要是再看到他的話，我一定能一眼就認出來，這我敢掛保證，只是要用言語形容他還真是沒辦法。」

「你確定他有這個門的鑰匙？」律師又問。

「親愛的老兄，我——」安費準備回答道。

P. 21

亞特森說：「是，我知道，我問的這些問題都有點奇怪，但你也看到了，我沒問簽支票的人是誰，因為我想我應該認識他。我只是想確定，你說的事情是真的。」

「這你已經說過啦！」安費有些不悅，「我跟你說的每一個細節都是千真萬確的事。沒錯，他是有門的鑰匙，而且不到一個星期之前，我又看到他用鑰匙開門。」

亞特森先生沒有作聲，陷入深思。

「看來我不應該多嘴的，這檔子事就甭再提了。」安費先生說。

「我完全同意，我們握個手、一言為定吧，理查。」律師回答。

尋找海德先生

P. 22

亞特森律師一個人住。在星期天用完晚餐後，他通常會坐在火爐邊看書，一直到教堂的午夜鐘聲響起，才會心懷感恩地上床就寢。這天晚上，他一如往常地吃著晚餐，心裡頭卻一直掛著安費所講的那件事情。晚餐過後，他沒有坐下來看書，而是走到他用來當辦公室的那個房間，然後從保險箱裡頭取出一份文件，只見外面的信封上寫著：「傑寇博士的遺囑」。

這份已經擬好的遺囑現在由亞特森先生全權負責，然而當初在撰寫時，他並不肯協助撰寫。遺囑上聲明，如果傑寇博士有什麼三長兩短，他所有的金錢和財產都歸「好友愛德華．海德」所有。還有，如果傑寇博士在任何情況下失蹤，或是無故消失三個月以上，海德先生就名正言順擁有傑寇博士的一切財產。

P. 23

身為律師的亞特森先生一點也不喜歡這份遺囑，加上現在又聽到有關那位海德先生的事，於是他就更加反感了。他以前覺得這種遺囑很愚蠢，現在覺得事有蹊蹺，恐怕牽涉到非法之事。

他決定立刻去找他的醫生朋友藍彥博士，博士也許可以告訴他更多的事情。他人一到，藍彥博士便招呼他走進飯廳，博士剛才正坐在裡頭獨飲葡萄酒。他們是同窗老友，大學時也是朋友，倆人互相景仰，很喜歡彼此的相伴。

在入座寒暄片刻後，亞特森先生開始切入正題，談到晚上來找藍彥的原因。

「我想我們兩個是亨利．傑寇最有交情的老朋友了吧！」他說。

「沒錯，不過我希望他的老朋友能年輕些，」藍彥打趣道：「你問這做什麼？這些日子以來，我很少和他碰面了。」

「是怎麼了？我還以為你們都對科學很有興趣呢！」亞特森問道。

「是沒錯，我們都很有興趣，更確切地說，是曾經臭味相投過。但是十年前我們就意見不合了，我覺得他愈走愈偏。當然基於老交情，我還是會繼續關心他，可是這傢伙的想法毫無科學根據，根本就是胡說八道。」博士回答。

「你有見過他一位叫做海德的朋友嗎？」亞特森先生提高了嗓音說道。

P. 24

「沒有，我沒聽說過這號人物。他一定是在我們互不來往之後，傑寇才結交的朋友。」藍彥博士答道。

在喝了一些酒，多聊了一會兒之後，亞特森先生打道回府。當晚他難以入眠，念念不忘這件聽來的事情，和他打探到的一些消息。

當隔壁那間教堂的鐘聲在清晨六點響起之際，亞特森仍在床上輾轉反側。安費說的那件事情一直盤據在他心頭。他擔心好友傑寇博士受到海德的影響，於是決定去探查海德先生的底細，揭開他的真面目，讓事情有個水落石出。那份奇怪的遺囑可能有其他隱情，而傑寇博士會和人見人嫌的海德先生交上朋友也一定事出有因。

所以從那天起，亞特森先生就常來街道的這道門觀察。

「如果他是『躲藏先生』，那我就是『尋找先生』了。」他邊想著，露出了一絲笑意。（譯註：「海德」（Hyde）和「躲藏」（hide）兩字發音相同）

之後，在一個乾冷的晚上，他的耐心終於有了代價。當時已過了晚上十點鐘，商店都拉下了大門，街上空無一人，非常安靜，只有城市遠處的熱鬧聲響還可以依稀可聞。

入夜之後到了此刻，一點點的聲響都會在寂靜的空氣中響徹遠方。亞特森這時聽到隱隱的腳步聲向他走近，他直覺這就是他想要打探的人，於是隱身到通往庭院的那條通道的暗處。他小心翼翼地從通道口往外望去，看到一個衣著普通的小個子男人走過來。即使當時兩人隔了一段距離，亞特森就覺得這個傢伙惹人討厭。

這傢伙直接走向大門，從口袋裡掏出了一把鑰匙。亞特森先生這時從暗處走出來，伸手碰了他的肩膀。

P. 26

「抱歉，我想你就是海德先生吧？」他說。

那人往退後了一步，整個人感覺更矮小了。「我就是海德。」他聲音很小，而且不敢正視亞特森，「請問閣下有何貴幹？」

「我叫亞特森，是傑寇博士的一個老朋友，我看你正要進去這屋子，所以想你可以也帶我進去！」

「傑寇博士不在這裡，你是怎麼知道我名字的？」這個矮小男人用很不友善的語氣回答道。

「你只要讓我看看你的臉，我就告訴你！」律師說道。

起初海德一動也不動，之後才臉轉向亞特森先生，兩人互相注視了片刻。

「如果我們再見面，我一定會認得你的。」亞特森先生說。

「能認識你是不錯，我應該給你我的住址。」他把蘇活區一條街道的門牌號碼告訴了亞特森先生。

這讓亞特森很意外。「他該不會想到那份遺囑了吧！」他暗忖：「或許他是要讓我知道可以去哪裡找他，這樣一來他要接收傑寇博士的遺產就更快了。」不過他沒有把這些告訴海德。

「現在可以說了吧！你是怎麼知道我的？」

「我們有共同的朋友，他們向我描述過閣下！」亞特森先生說。

「是誰？」海德突然大聲詰問起來。

「比方說，傑寇博士。」

「他才從沒告訴過你這些！」海德氣沖沖地說：「想不到你這樣撒謊。」

他很快地打開大門，隱身進入屋裡。

P. 27

海德的反應

- 海德似乎知道亞特森沒有實話實說。為什麼海德知道傑寇博士沒有跟亞特森說過他的事？請兩人一組進行探討，想想原因究竟為何！

一臉困惑的亞特森先生呆立了許久，然後才緩緩地走開。他皺著眉頭，不時駐足下來，陷入了沉思之中。的確，海德先生長得醜陋、討人厭，但又說不上來他到底是哪裡長得醜。連他的聲音也很不悅耳，一付破鑼嗓子。除此之外還有一些怪怪的地方，但亞特森先生無法立刻指出來，或許只是因為他的個性很討人厭，所以他的樣子和舉止無形中也就變得令人討厭了。海德給人的感覺很邪門，一想到老友傑寇博士竟然和這種人做朋友，亞特森便不由得感到憂心。

從那扇門的側街轉過街角，會來到另一處街區，那邊的房子雖然老舊，但是蓋得不錯，現在大多都已分割成一間間的公寓，但當中有一棟房子還是完整，是獨棟獨戶的。亞特森先生敲了敲大門，一位衣著整齊的老僕人出來應門。

P. 28

「晚安，卜爾，傑寇博士在嗎？」律師問。

「亞特森先生，我去看一下，請進來坐好嗎？」卜爾回答。

亞特森先生走進屋內氣派的大廳，在開放式的壁爐旁等候，爐內火光灼灼。在倫敦，這個大廳大概是他最喜歡的房間了！但亞特森先生此時憂心忡忡，他並不期待和好友傑寇博士攤開講這件事。這時僕人走進來，表示傑寇博士不在家，亞特森先生聽到時鬆了口氣。

「我在轉角看見海德先生從後門走進屋子，傑寇博士不在家，這樣沒問題嗎？」律師問。

「沒問題！亞特森先生，海德先生有鑰匙！」僕人回答。

「那麼說，傑寇博士很信任這個人囉？」

「是的，先生，的確是，我們奉命要服從他。只是海德先生很少出現在屋子的這邊，甚至從未留下來用過晚餐，他通常都是由後面的實驗室大門進出。」

「好吧，卜爾，那我先告辭了。」

「晚安，亞特森先生。」

亞特森離開時不由得心想：「可憐的亨利．傑寇，他是年少輕狂過，但我想他現在交了海德這種損友，才更可怕呢。海德大概和傑寇過去幹過的荒唐事有關連，雖然是陳年往事了，但有些事情是一輩子也擺脫不掉的。我想海德自己也有不可告人的可怕祕密，一想到他竟像個賊一樣偷偷闖入亨利的生活中，我就不由得不寒而慄。不知道海德對那份遺囑的事情到底知道多少，是否知道他可以這麼簡單就能繼承到亨利．傑寇的財產。我就一定要想個辦法，傑寇要是肯讓我插手的話。」

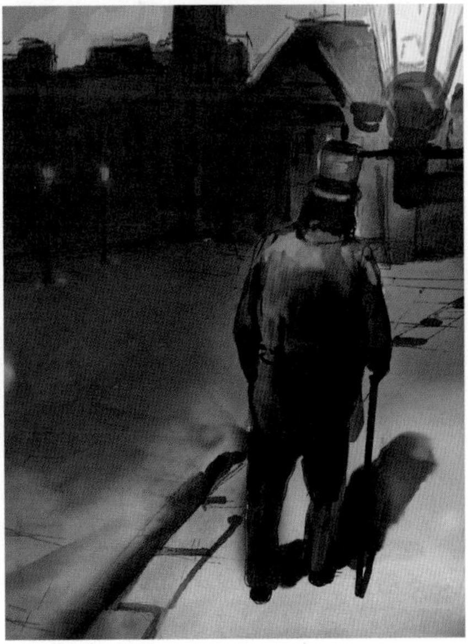

傑寇博士輕鬆以對

P.30

兩個星期之後，傑寇博士約了三五個好友到家中吃大餐，其中包括了亞特森先生。當其他人都陸續離開後，他留了下來。他不是第一次待得這麼晚，而且這次這兩個朋友又像往常一樣，輕鬆愜意地坐在火爐的兩側，享受靜謐。現在機會終於來了，亞特森先生可以問問海德和遺囑的事。

「傑寇，我想和你談談，你知道那份遺囑的事吧？」他問道。

傑寇博士猶豫了一下，然後神情愉快地回答說：「我想你有了我這樣差勁的委託人。我知道你很不喜歡這份遺囑，我惹火了你，更是惹火了藍彥博士。」傑寇看來是想轉移話題：「他老是跟我在科學上的觀點唱反調，我對他很失望。」

「你也知道，我對那份遺囑充滿了疑惑。」亞特森說道，不跟他談藍彥博士的事。

「我知道，你之前說過！」傑寇的語氣變得尖銳起來。

「那我就再說一遍，因為我最近查到了一些海德先生的事。」

傑寇博士收起笑容，臉色變得很蒼白，「我們不是說好不談這個話題的嗎！」

「但是我聽到了一些不是很好的事。」

「沒事的。你不了解我的處境，聊天也不能解決問題。」傑寇博士心平氣和地說。

p.31

「傑寇，你知道你可以相信我的。發生了什麼事，你就跟我說吧。」

「亞特森，我知道你是一番好意，沒錯，這世界上我最可以信任的人就是你了，但事情沒有你想像的壞。為了讓你放心，我可以跟你一件事：只要我願意，我隨時都可以擺脫海德先生，這一點我可以向你保證。感謝你的關心，但求求你，這是私事，就別再提了，拜託，甚至連想都不要再想了。」

亞特森先生望著火爐，不發一語，最後才說道：「沒錯，我想你是一定沒什麼問題的。」說完，他起身準備離去。

「你提到了海德，我希望以後永遠不要再談到他，我只想說，我和可憐的海德有很深切的關係。他跟我說，你曾經見過他，也跟我說了你們的事。我想他是很粗魯，但我希望你可以答應我，幫助他得到他應有的權益。你要是肯點頭，我會更高興的。」傑寇說道。

亞特森嘆了口氣說道：「我沒辦法假裝我喜歡他這個人，但，好吧，亨利，我答應你。」

克魯凶殺案

P.32

大約過了一年之後，時值十月，有一位大人物——國會議員在倫敦慘遭殺害。有一個女僕目睹了這樁犯罪案件，當時約晚上十一點，月光皎潔，她從自家窗戶向外眺望，看到一位頭髮灰白、身材高大的老紳士正沿著街道步行，另外有一位個頭較矮的男人從對面走過來。

兩人隨後在她的窗戶下方打了照面，她看到老紳士鞠了一躬，接著聽到他向對方說了一些話，她認出了另一人就是海德先生，因為海德曾經拜訪過她的雇主一次。高大的老紳士友善地向他欠身致意，彬彬有禮地好像是在跟他問路，未料矮個子卻突然脾氣大發，用他那根沉甸甸的手杖開始猛擊白髮老紳士。

P. 33

根據女僕的說詞，那凶惡的男人「像個瘋子似的」，一直打老紳士，直到對方倒在地上才罷手，然後海德又用腳對著老人猛踢猛踩。女僕這時還聽到骨頭碎裂的聲音，接著她就嚇暈了過去。

當她清醒過來時，已經午夜兩點，於是她叫來了警察，當時海德早已溜掉，只剩高大老人血肉模糊的屍體橫躺在地上。海德用來行凶的那根手杖，在猛力攻擊時斷成兩半，其中半截掉落在屍首旁邊，另外半截被凶手隨手帶走。警察到達現場後，在老人的口袋中發現了一些錢和一只金錶，另外還有一個信封，上面寫著的是亞特森先生的地址。

當天一大早，警察便帶著那個信封前往律師的住處，當時律師還尚未起床。在未看到屍體之前，亞特森先生不作任何發言。他後來認出死者是丹佛．克魯爵士，他是一位大名鼎鼎且備受尊崇的國會議員。

警方這時才了解到這是一樁重大案件，並要求亞特森協助找出凶手。他們把女僕所目睹到的情況告訴他，而且表示她知道凶手的大名。當警方提到海德這個名字時，亞特森就不禁打了個冷顫。接著警方又把現場那半截斷裂的手杖拿給他看，他認出來那是多年前他送給傑寇博士的手杖！現在事實明擺了女僕所看到的「海德先生」，和他所認識的海德先生一定是同一個人。

P. 34

「你們跟我走，我可以帶各位到這位海德先生的住所。」他跟警方說道。

上午九點左右，他們一行人就坐著一輛出租馬車，穿過濃霧，來到海德曾寫給亞特森的一處蘇活區地址。待濃霧消散了些後，他們看到那裡是倫敦市的一處貧民窟，看來傑寇的繼承人就住在這個地方，等著繼承傑寇的二萬五千英鎊遺產。

他們敲了大門，來應門的是一位銀髮婦人。婦人很有禮貌，但沒幫上什麼忙。沒錯，海德先生是住在這裡，但他昨晚上很晚才回來，而且一下子就又出門了。

「這位是蘇格蘭警場的紐柯曼探長，我們想看一下海德的房間。」亞特森說道。

P. 36

「哦，他闖禍了嗎？」婦人臉上露出陰沉的一笑，「他捅了什麼簍子？」

「只要讓我們進去看看就好。」探長說。

「看來這個海德的人緣很差。」探長小聲地對亞特森說道。

他們走進房間，發現偌大的屋子裡雖然有許多房間，但海德只用到其中的兩間，接著又看到房間裡都是上好的傢俱，有些還很豪華。他們看到，這兩個房間剛被倉促地搜過，抽屜不但打開著，裡頭的東西也扔得整個房間都是；地板上到處都是衣服，衣服的口袋都被翻了出來。

冰冷的壁爐裡還有一堆灰燼，紐柯曼探長在灰燼裡找到一本支票簿的殘骸；那裡還有斷裂的一截手杖，靠在門後的牆上。紐柯曼探長判定，這半截手杖證明了海德就是凶手。

P. 37

由於他在灰燼裡找到了支票簿，於是決定前往海德的銀行一探究竟。當他們到達銀行，和銀行經理談過之後，發現了海德的帳戶裡有數千英鎊。

「我們現在可以很快尋線找到他了，他一定在情急之下慌了，不然怎麼會笨得把支票簿燒掉，又留下半截手杖等著我們去發現。當然，生活上是少不了錢的，我們只要在銀行守株待兔，再放話出去，讓每個人都知道我們正在找他就行了。」警員說道。

不過，說起來容易，做起來就不是那麼回事。認識海德的人屈指可數，而且沒有任何人有他的照片。他們也無法聯繫上他的家人，而且大家對他的描繪又多有出入，唯一相符的證詞就是：他看起來就是怪怪的，卻又很難形容是哪裡怪怪的，而且讓人一眼難忘。

一封信件所帶來的小插曲

P. 38

在那天傍晚左右，亞特森先生又來到了傑寇博士的房子，僕人卜爾開門讓他進去，帶他穿過房子，經過庭院，來到後方那間用來當實驗室的屋子。

這是亞特森第一次見到這間實驗室，他看到房子沒有窗戶，而且看起來很髒亂，裡頭到處散落著化學儀器和大紙箱。在房間的另一頭有一個樓梯，通向一扇紅色的門，那裡就是傑寇博士的私人辦公室。

這間辦公室很大，裡面的擺設有櫃子、一片大鏡子、一個壁爐和一盞油燈，裡面有三扇緊閉的窗戶，向外眺望可以看到庭院。亞特森看到傑寇博士坐在爐火邊，一付病懨懨的樣子。傑寇伸出一隻冷冰冰的手，用虛弱的聲音問候他。

「你聽到凶殺案的新聞了嗎？」等卜爾一走，亞特森先生便忙不迭地問道。

「聽到了，我聽到外頭有人在高聲闊論地談這件事，從飯廳就可以聽到了」。

「克魯是我的委託人，而你也是，我想知道這件事會對我有什麼影響，所以一定要問個清楚，你該不會笨到去窩藏海德先生這位殺人凶手吧？」亞特森說。

P. 39

「我敢對天發誓，我再也不會和他見面了，我和他已經一刀兩斷，我可以向你保證，決不會再和他有任何瓜葛。」博士說。

「我真心希望你說得沒錯！」律師說道。

「有件事得要你提供些意見，我收到了一封信，不知道是否應該交給警方。我信任你，所以想把信交給你，至於該怎麼辦就由你決定好了。」傑寇說道。

傑寇遞給亞特森一張紙，信上的筆跡拉得又長又直，看起來很怪異，署名者是海德。信上說，長久以來傑寇博士一直待他不薄，自己卻不知感恩圖報，但傑寇博士不會受到波及，而他自己有十足的把握可以逃脫。

P. 40

讀完這封信之後，亞特森覺得好過了些，海德似乎並不想讓他的朋友傑寇受到任何傷害，他之前對海德的懷疑並不完全正確。

「你有信封嗎？」亞特森問。

「沒有，我一時沒有想到它很重要，就把它燒掉了，不過上面沒有郵戳，信是塞在大門邊的。」

「我再想想看這封信應該怎麼處置。告訴我，你遺囑上有段話提到你失蹤後要怎麼處理，那是不是海德叫你寫的？」亞特森說。

傑寇博士沒有說話，但點了點頭。「這還真讓我學到了一個教訓！」他大聲說道。

「我想也是，他想謀殺你，還好你逃過了這一劫。」

亞特森在離開時，問卜爾當天是否有人送一封信來，但卜爾表示，他很確定沒有看到什麼信。

這讓亞特森又憂心了起來，如果那封信不是送到前門的話，就一定是塞在實驗室的大門，甚至信還有可能是在實驗室裡寫好的。要是這樣的話，他處理這件事就要更小心了。

他一趕回家裡，便和他的主任祕書蓋斯特先生一同坐在火爐邊討論，他常和這位主任祕書討論私密的事情。蓋斯特先生認識傑寇博士，也聽過海德先生這號人物，而且他還是筆跡專家。

亞特森決定跟蓋斯特透露，說他手上有一封由丹佛爵士案凶手所親筆寫的信件，他想把信拿給他看。他知道蓋斯特會一邊看信，一邊說出自己的想法。

P. 41

「沒錯，丹佛．克魯爵士遇刺一事真讓人感到難過，凶手當然一定是個瘋子。」蓋斯特說。

「我想聽聽你對這件事的看法，我這裡有一份凶手親筆寫的信。就是這個，這是凶手的筆跡。」亞特森說。

蓋斯特立刻坐下來，開始認真研究起來。

「亞特森先生，他寫字的風格很怪異，不過，不對，我覺得寫這封信的人並沒有發瘋。」

「是沒錯，不管怎麼說，會寫這種字的人是一個怪人。」蓋斯特補充道。

就在這個時候，亞特森的僕人走了進來，帶來傑寇博士邀請亞特森共進晚餐的短箋。

「我可以看嗎？」蓋斯特說。「謝謝，很有意思，這封信和短箋的筆跡很像，只是書寫的斜度有些不同罷了。」

「這個巧合真令人意外。」亞特森說。

「沒錯，太巧了！」蓋斯特十分認同。

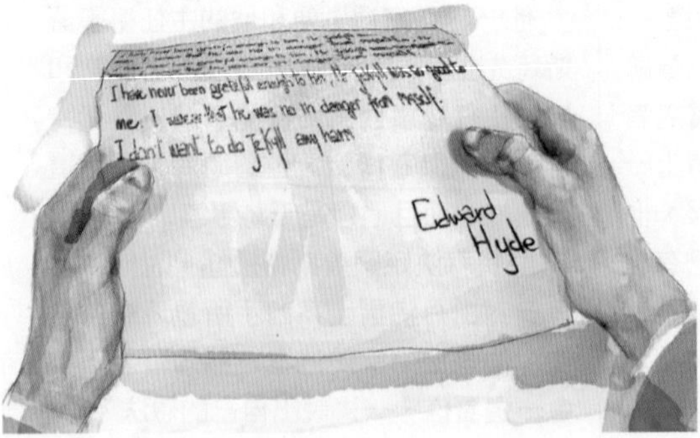

「蓋斯特，這份短箋我是不會對任何人提起的，你明白吧？」

「當然不可以，先生，我明白！」

亞特森把短箋另外鎖起來，他想不通傑寇為何要冒用凶手的名字寫信，「為什麼他要替一名凶手掩飾？」他心想，不禁打冷顫。

藍彥博士的驚人意外

P. 42

丹佛．克魯爵士的凶殺案成了市內的大新聞，由於爵士備受尊崇，因此慘遭殺害的消息讓許多人憤憤不平。只要有人能向警方提供海德的藏身之處，就可以獲得數千英鎊的巨額懸賞，但沒有人知道他的行蹤，他完全消失了蹤跡。

一陣子之後，亞特森先生回復了平日的生活，丹佛爵士遇難的傷痛，也由於海德的行蹤不明而得以平復。如今邪惡的海德似乎已從這個世界上徹底消失。

傑寇博士的生活也變得比較好了，他三不五時就忙著外出和朋友吃飯。有兩個月左右的時間，他似乎過得很愜意、很滿足。

一月八日這一天，傑寇、亞特森和兩人的好友藍彥博士一起用餐，三個人像是回到了昔日時光，再次相處融洽。亞特森差不多每天都會去探望好友傑寇，因此他隔天決定再訪。不過這回他沒有見到傑寇，因為卜爾在門口告訴他，博士在房間裡，不見任何人。

之後他又試了幾回，想見見老友，不過卻一再吃閉門羹。到了第六個晚上，亞特森先生改而探望藍彥博士。

P. 43

到了藍彥那裡，事情並沒有比較好。他雖然沒有被拒於門外，但當他一踏進屋子，吃了一大驚，因為藍彥臉色慘白，身子骨明顯虛弱許多，一付不久於人世的樣子。藍彥變得更瘦、更禿，一下子蒼老許多，眼神中充滿了恐懼。

「我受到了可怕的驚嚇，永遠都無法復原了。」藍彥說。

「傑寇也生病了，你有看到他嗎？」亞特森問。

「我再也不想聽到或看到這個人！不要再提他了。」藍彥叫道。

亞特森先生沉默了一會兒後說道：「有什麼事是我可以做的嗎？我們三個都是老朋友了，我們這一生也沒有多少時間可以再認識別的老朋友了。」

「做什麼事都沒有用，什麼都沒有用，去問傑寇吧。」

「他不肯見我！」亞特森答道。

「我想也是，等我死了，你就會發現到底發生了什麼事，但我現在無法告訴你。如果你想繼續待下來，就換個話題；如果你一定要談這件事，那就請回吧！」藍彥說。

亞特森後來回到家時，就坐下來寫了封信給傑寇，問他為什麼不想見他，為什麼要和藍彥絕交。第二天，他收到了傑寇長長的一封回信，而且回覆的內容很奇怪。

P. 44

傑寇在信上表示，他沒有責怪藍彥的意思，但承認他們永遠都不應該再見面了。他說自己做錯了一件事，從今以後再也不見任何人了。他沒有交待原因，只是表示今後會過著與世隔絕的生活。他在信中寫道，亞特森仍然是他的好朋友，但如果他閉門不見，亞特森也不應該感到意外。他做了一件極大的錯事，應該接受懲罰才對，他要亞特森尊重他的意願。

亞特森先生很訝異，惡棍海德已經離開，每件事似乎都逐漸好轉，而且傑寇看起來很快樂。但如今，亞特森搞不懂為什麼每件事情在一個星期之內就都變調了。

一個星期之後，藍彥博士一病不起，不到兩個星期之後便與世長辭。在葬禮之後的那個晚上，亞特森先生把自己鎖在辦公室裡，傷心地拿出藍彥的遺囑，偌大的信封上寫著：「私密信件：J.G. 亞特森親啟，如果他不幸過世，請勿拆閱，並逕行銷毀。」

包覆在外面的大信封裡，還有另一個信封，上面出現這樣的字：「在亨利・

傑寇博士死亡或失蹤之前，不得拆閱」。

亞特森先生簡直不敢相信自己的眼睛，沒錯，是有「失蹤」這個字眼，而且又扯上了傑寇博士這個名字。藍彥的這份遺囑和傑寇的遺囑很相像，不久之前，亞特森才把傑寇的遺囑交還回去。他想到傑寇有可能失蹤（他有好一段時間沒見到傑寇了），這個念頭讓他想起了可怕的海德先生。

P. 46

這到底是怎麼回事？藍彥為什麼要寫這樣一份遺囑？亞特森身為律師，委託人所交付的祕密和規矩他都要謹遵不違。此刻他很想打破規矩，逕自開啟信封，但最後還是決定遵守職業規範，把亡友的這份遺囑放回隱密的保險櫃中。

他仍繼續三不五時地想要探望傑寇，但當傑寇博士的僕人卜爾拒他於門外時，亞特森反而有一種如釋重負之感。在他的內心深處，或許寧願站在台階上和卜爾聊一聊，也不想進入傑寇為自己打造的牢籠裡。

卜爾告訴亞特森，博士比以前更變本加厲了，整天都待在實驗室上面的辦公室裡，甚至有時候就在裡頭過夜。傑寇博士都是一付悶悶不樂的樣子，常常一語不發，甚至連書都不看了。因為卜爾所說的內容都差不多，久而久之，亞特森先生的拜訪次數就愈來愈少了。

窗口的奇遇

P. 48

在一個星期天，亞特森先生一如往常地和安費先生一起散步。他們再次沿著側街閒逛，當兩人來到那扇大門前的時候，不約而同地駐足觀看。安費先生說：「事情最後總算是落幕了，海德再也不會出現了，真是感謝老天。」

「但願再也不會見到他。」亞特森說：「我有沒有告訴過你，我曾和他打過一次照面，而且和你一樣也覺得他的樣子很討人厭？」

「每個人對他都是這種感覺，任誰看到他，都會有這樣的感覺。」安費說道：「對啦，你一定會認為我是個笨蛋，竟然不知道這扇門正是通往傑寇博士家的後門。」

「所以這麼說來，你也發現到了，對不對？如果是這樣的話，那現在何不乾脆穿過這個入口，進入庭院裡，看看可不可以在窗口上看到傑寇，反正我們都已經走到這裡了！」亞特森說。

庭院裡冷颼颼的，而且很陰暗，即使

現在是豔陽高照的大白天。在二樓的中間有扇半掩的窗戶，他們抬頭仰望，赫然看見傑寇博士一臉愁容地坐在窗前，凝視著外面的庭院。

P. 49

「喂，傑寇！我想你一定好多了吧！」亞特森先生扯開嗓門叫道。

「我不是很好，一點也沒有比較好，看來我日子不久了，感謝上帝！」傑寇答道。

「你老是待在屋子裡，應該出來走走，就像我的表弟安費先生和我這樣。順便給你們介紹一下，安費，這位是傑寇先生；傑寇，這是安費先生。」律師說道。

他們兩人互相點了點頭。

「亨利，來吧！穿上你的大衣，戴好帽子，跟我們一起走走吧，只要一會兒就好。」

「你的好意我心領了，真高興見到你們兩位，我也很想和你們一起散散步，但那是不可能的事，我不敢出去。我也很想邀請你和安費進來坐坐，可是這房子實在不適合讓訪客進來。」

「既然這樣，那我們就站在這裡和你聊聊就好！」律師笑著拉高了嗓門說。

P. 50

「我正想這樣提議呢！」傑寇也笑著回答。

然而他話才一說完，他的笑臉就陡然消失，變成一臉的驚懼神色，讓站在下面庭院的兩位朋友看得直打冷顫。冷不防地，傑寇博士砰的一聲把窗戶關上，消失在兩人的眼前。

亞特森和安費穿過入口離去，沿著側街而行，他們一路上還很震驚，半句話都說不上來。一陣子之後，他們來到市區一處繁忙熱鬧的地方，亞特森這時才放聲喊道：「願上帝饒恕我們！」

安費先生臉色沉重，沒有說什麼，只是點了點頭，接著兩人又帶著哀傷地靜靜往前走去。

亞特森

- 如果你遇見了亞特森，你會想問他什麼問題？和夥伴一起詢問這些問題，並討論亞特森可能會做出什麼答覆。

最後一夜

P. 51

這天晚上，亞特森先生在家用過晚餐，正坐在火爐邊時，傑寇博士的僕人卜爾來訪，讓他甚感意外。

「卜爾，是什麼風把你給吹來了？」亞特森喊道：「難道是博士病了嗎？」

「亞特森先生，有些事不太對勁。」僕人說。

「坐下來，卜爾，先來杯葡萄酒。現在，慢慢把發生的事情詳詳細細地告訴我！」

「先生，你也知道博士的情況，他會把自己給關在辦公室裡，他現在又把自己關在辦公室裡了，我不喜歡他這樣，我很害怕。」卜爾說。

「卜爾，你這話是什麼意思？你在怕什麼？」

「先生，他這樣子已經一個星期左右了！」卜爾沒有回答亞特森的問題，「我再也受不了！」

卜爾的神情說出了他的恐懼。他無助地坐著，兩眼盯著屋角，他沒有碰葡萄酒，也不直視律師的臉。

「好，我可以看出來，情況的確很不對勁，現在告訴我究竟是怎麼回事？」亞特森說。

「我不敢說，但我想發生了很恐怖的事情，可否勞您大駕親自來看看，先生？」卜爾的聲音裡充滿了恐懼。

P.52

亞特森很快取來大衣和帽子，他注意到卜爾的臉上充滿了感激的表情，又發現卜爾仍沒有碰那杯葡萄酒。

他們快步走過冷風颼颼的倫敦夜晚，月色蒼冷，街上異乎尋常地空無一人，塵土在強風下四處飛揚，並不是一個適合外出的夜晚。

當他們到達傑寇博士的住處時，卜爾在人行道的中間停下來，用充滿畏懼的聲音說道：「先生，我們到了，希望沒出什麼差錯才好！」

卜爾謹慎地敲了門，扣著門鏈的大門應聲打開，只見一個受到驚嚇的女僕悄聲問道：「卜爾，是你嗎？」

卜爾答道：「沒事，你可以開門。」

大廳裡聚集了傑寇博士的一大群僕人，他們站在明亮的爐火前，看起來就像一群羊群，而且個個神情緊張。

「感謝老天，是亞特森先生！」廚子一邊喊道，一邊跑向亞特森，做勢要擁抱他。

「怎麼回事？你們怎麼都聚在這裡？這樣太奇怪了，傑寇博士看到你們這樣會怎麼說？」亞特森喊道。

卜爾答道：「他們嚇壞了！亞特森先生，請跟我過來！」卜爾拿著蠟燭，帶他走到後花園，朝實驗室走去。

「現在請小聲點，千萬別讓他知道您在這裡！您只要仔細聽動靜就好，不要說話，萬一他要你進辦公室的話，你千萬不要進去！」卜爾說。

P.53

卜爾的話讓他感到吃驚，他跟著走進實驗室，來到最裡頭的樓梯腳邊。卜爾要亞特森站在那裡，然後一個人緩緩步上樓梯，來到大門邊，神色驚恐。

「先生，亞特森來了，他想見您！」卜爾對著緊閉的門說道。

「跟他說，我誰都不能見！」門後傳了不悅的聲音。

「謝謝您，先生！」卜爾答道，彷彿他很高興聽到這個回答似的。接著他帶著亞特森經過花園，回到主屋的大廚房裡。

進到廚房後，卜爾盯著亞特森的眼睛，表情嚴肅地問道：「先生，那是我主人的聲音嗎？」

「他的聲音聽起來很不一樣。」亞特森臉色蒼白，盯著卜爾的眼睛回答道。

「我在傑寇博士這裡工作了二十年，應該不會認錯他的聲音。我想博士遭到殺害了，而且八天前就被殺害了，我們聽到了他大叫的聲音。現在，待在辦公室裡的，到底是誰？他是什麼怪東西？這個怪東西……為什麼會待在裡面不走？我們想弄清楚！」

「卜爾，這聽起來很詭異，太奇怪了。如果……我只是假設，如果傑寇博士已經遇害，那凶手為什麼要待在裡面不走，這很不合理。」亞特森說。

P.55

卜爾答道：「亞特森先生，你是個很難被說服的人。我跟你說，不管現在在辦公室裡的是誰或是什麼怪東西，他已經在裡面待了一個星期了，而且還會嚷著要買什麼藥的。傑寇博士有時會把指示給寫在紙上，留在樓梯口。這個星期以來，辦公室的門都關著，只有一些紙條，丟在樓梯口那裡。我每天都要出去兩三趟，等我跑遍市區的藥房、把他要的藥買回來，就又會收到新的紙條，說藥的成份不純，要把我藥退還回去，再去別家藥局買。先生，不管他想要用那些藥來做什麼，那些藥量都很多。」

「你有留下那些紙條嗎？」亞特森問。

卜爾把手伸進口袋裡，交給他一張被揉得皺巴巴的紙，上面有寫給藥房的內容，表示不論價錢有多貴，他都要到拿到一種「成份純正、古法製造的藥」。到了字條最後，冷靜自然的口吻突然變得很激動，最後一行寫著：「搞什麼鬼啊，快給我找古法製造的藥！」

「這很奇怪！」亞特森先是平靜地說道，接著尖銳地問道：「信怎麼沒有封起來？怎麼被打開了？」

「先生，因為藥房的人看了很生氣，把信扔還給我，所以我就好把它撿起來，然後帶回家。」

「你確定這是博士的筆跡？」亞特森問道。

P.56

「我覺得這很像他的筆跡，不過這不是很重要，因為我看到他的人了。」

「你看到他的人了？」亞特森重覆問說道：「是嗎？」

「是，有一天我從花園來到實驗室，撞見了他在樓梯口。那時他已經走出辦公室一會兒，他抬頭看到我時，叫了一聲，接著一溜煙地鑽回辦公室。我那時只撞見了他一下下，但他的樣子讓我汗毛直豎。如果他就是我家主人的話，那麼他臉上一定是戴上了面具，因為他的臉看起來都不一樣了！還有，如果那就是他，他為什麼要發出叫聲，然後鑽回辦公室裡來躲我？我都替他工作這麼多年了。」

亞特森答道：「這的確很奇怪，但我開始看出一些眉目了，我想你家主人傑寇博士大概是患了什麼很痛的病，而且會讓他的長相變形。這樣就可以解釋他為什麼會大叫一聲，也可以解釋為什麼連老朋友都不想見，還有他的聲音也都變了，所以急著買藥讓自己好起來。」

「先生，那個傢伙不是我家主人，這是很明確的事實，傑寇博士又高又帥，但這傢伙又矮又醜。」卜爾堅持己見地說。

卜爾又繼續說：「我可以保證那一定不是他，這二十年來，我每天早上都會看到主人，難道你認為我還不認識他？不知道他人長得多高？不可能，戴面具的傢伙不是傑寇，我想博士已經遇害了。」

P. 57

傑寇博士

- 你覺得傑寇博士到底發生了什麼事？和夥伴一起討論。

「卜爾，既然你這麼認為，那我就查個水落石出。這張紙條顯示傑寇還活著，我有責任闖進辦公室，查出事實真相。」

「沒錯，沒錯，這是應該要這麼做。」卜爾喊道。

「那誰要來破門而入？」亞特森問道。

「先生，當然是你和我一起闖進去！」卜爾忙不迭地這樣回答。

「我有斧頭，」卜爾繼續說道：「你要我到廚房裡幫你拿根火鉗嗎？」

亞特森拿起火鉗，說道：「卜爾，你和我等一下可能會有點危險，我們應該要互相坦誠，我們兩人的心裡有些話並沒有說出來。你看過那個戴面具的傢伙了，你等會兒可以認出他來嗎？」

「當時事情發生得太快了，我沒有十足的把握，不過你要是問說那個傢伙是否就是海德先生，那我會說是，我覺得他就是海德，他們身材差不多，而且除了他，還有誰可以從實驗室的大門進去？在那件命案發生時，海德先生都還握有鑰匙。事情還不止如此，亞特森先生，你看過海德嗎？」

「我看過，而且和他說過一次話。」

「那你一定知道這個傢伙就是很怪，讓人打從心底發毛。」

「是沒錯，我也有這種感覺。」

P. 58

「就是這樣，先生，當我一看到那個傢伙時，感覺就是這樣，覺得脊背發冷，我敢發誓，那個傢伙就是海德先生！」

「我想也是這樣，可憐的亨利可能已經遇害，而凶手就在辦公室裡消遙法外。我們現在就來看看我們說得對不對。」亞特森說。

他們又找來兩位僕人繞到後面的大門守住，以防有人脫逃。亞特森跟他們說，他和卜爾會等個十分鐘，好讓他們就定位。

接著亞特森又說：「卜爾，我們現在也各就各位！」

他帶著卜爾穿過花園，朝實驗室走去。此時暮色漆黑，四周靜悄悄的，燭火被風吹得搖曳不定，把他們的影子投射在花園裡。因為四下無聲，他們能聽得到辦公室裡走來走去的輕盈腳步聲。

「這不是傑寇博士的腳步聲，腳步太輕了。」亞特森說。

「他整天都這樣走來走去，只有新藥送來的時候才會停下腳步。」卜爾說道。

「他還有什麼其他的動靜嗎？」亞特森問道。

卜爾點點頭，說：「有，我有一次聽到他在哭，哭得很像女人、很崩潰，哭聲聽起來很悽慘，讓我聽了都想跟著哭。」

十分鐘的時間轉眼已過，卜爾拎起斧頭，和亞特森悄悄地接近大門，屏住呼吸。

「傑寇，讓我看看你。」亞特森喊道。

P. 60

他等了一會兒，但是沒有回應。

「我再說一次，我一定要見你，一定要看到你，如果你不開門，我們就要硬闖了。」他又大聲喊道。

「亞特森，你就可憐可憐我吧，拜託！」裡頭終於有了回應。

「這不是傑寇的聲音，是海德的聲音！」亞特森對卜爾說。

接著他們開始破門而入，卜爾把斧頭舉過肩頭，然後使勁往大門劈去，力道大得整棟房子都作響，但門只凹進去了一些些。卜爾又揮舞斧頭，劈向大門的木製鑲板。連揮了四次以上之後，門鎖應聲斷裂，建造結實的大門向後倒塌在辦公室裡。

這時一切都靜了下來，兩人為自己的粗暴行徑感到吃驚，接著穿過洞開的門，小心翼翼地往屋子裡查看。

乍看之下，裡頭似乎一切如常，一盞油燈把辦公室照得明亮，壁爐裡燒著熊熊烈火，前方有一只正燒著水的茶壺，旁邊還放置了一些飲茶的器具；裡頭有兩個打開的抽屜，書桌上有一疊放得整整齊齊的紙張；裡頭靜悄悄的，除了幾個櫃子裡放了一些粉狀物和化學藥品之外，一切都普通得和倫敦任何地方的辦公室一樣。

然而當他們再仔細一瞧，發現房間的中央有一個怪怪的東西。有一個男人面部朝下地躺在地上，全身微微抽搐著。他們把他的身體翻過來，認出那是愛德華．海德先生的臉，他穿著一身又寬又大的衣服，衣服的大小是博士的尺寸。

P.62

他的身體雖然微微抽動，但那是死亡之後肌肉和神經的抽動而已，已經沒有生命的氣息。他的手裡握著一個小玻璃瓶，瓶子裡散發一股類似於苦杏仁的獨特氣味。亞特森知道這是什麼味道，那是砒霜這種致命毒物的味道，海德服毒自殺了。

「我們來晚了一步，不管是要救他還是懲罰他，都為時已遲，海德已經自殺了，如今我們還得找到傑寇博士的屍體。」亞特森說。

他們在辦公室、實驗室、走廊、寬敞的地下室，以及建築物中的各個小房間展開徹底的搜索，可是不論亨利·傑寇是死是活，到處都找不到蹤跡。

「搞不好他把他埋了！」卜爾踩了踩走廊的石板，仔細聽著是否有中空的聲音。

「他也可能已經逃走了，」亞特森邊說邊注視通往屋外側街的大門，「但門是鎖著的。」

接著，他們在大門旁邊找到了鑰匙。鑰匙生鏽了，而且都斷了，顯然有很長的一段時間沒有使用了。

「鑰匙好像是被人用力踩斷的。」卜爾說。

「沒錯，斷裂面也都生鏽了。卜爾，我看不出什麼眉目，我們先回辦公室吧！」

P.63

他們回到辦公室進行地毯式搜查，心裡頭很困惑，而且憂心。他們在桌子上看到用來做實驗的化學藥品，看來這個鬱鬱寡歡的人曾把幾小堆的白鹽仔細計量過，然後放置在小玻璃板上，準備進行實驗。

「這和我買給他的藥一樣！」卜爾說道。

壁爐旁茶壺裡的水此時剛好沸騰，他們看到安樂椅旁邊擺著一個茶杯，杯裡已經放好了糖。旁邊還放了傑寇博士喜歡看的書本，可是在敞開的那一頁上，卻寫滿了憤世嫉俗的話，字跡十分潦草。他們又看到了一面大鏡子，鏡面朝天花板。接著，他們來到書桌前，上面整整齊齊地堆了一疊文件。

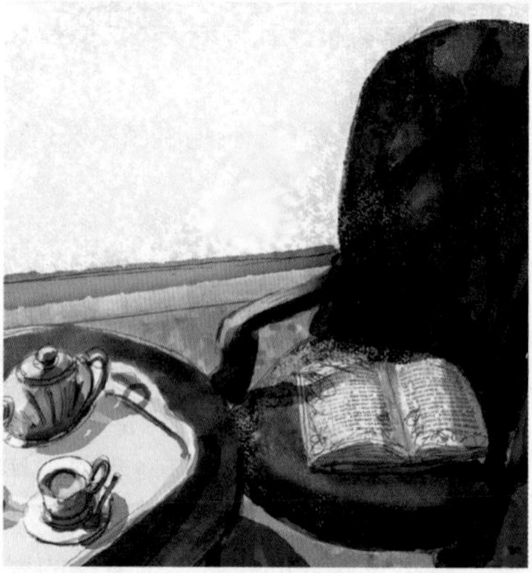

P.64

擺放在最上面的文件，是一個大信封，上面寫著亞特森先生的名字，那是傑寇博士的筆跡。律師把信打開，裡頭掉出來了幾個小信封，其中有一封是傑寇博士新立的遺囑。新遺囑和之前的一樣，是一些稀奇古怪的條款，但有一個很重要的差別。上一份是交待由海德先生繼承傑寇博士的財產和金錢，但這次傑寇寫的是另一個姓名：加柏瑞．約翰．亞特森。

亞特森很吃驚，他抬頭看了看卜爾，接著目光回到遺囑上，之後望向地板的屍體。

「我真不敢相信，海德竟然拿到了這份遺囑，他看到自己的名字被換成了我的名字，一定很生氣，恨透了我，但他竟然沒有把遺囑銷毀掉。」亞特森說。

接著，他看了看第二份文件，那是一份短箋，上面寫的日期是今天，那是傑寇博士的筆跡。

「卜爾，一直到今天，博士還活著，而且就待在這裡。他不可能在這麼短的時間裡被殺害，然後屍體就被移走。他還活著，一定是逃走了，要是這樣，那海德真的是自殺的嗎？還是被傑寇博士所殺的？我們一定要小心行事，不然可能會給博士帶來更多的麻煩。」亞特森說。

P. 65

「先生，您怎麼不看看短箋裡面寫了什麼？」卜爾建議說。

「我不太敢看裡面寫什麼，希望我的顧慮是多餘的。」亞特森說。

亞特森看著短箋，上面寫著：

亞特森先生：

當你看到這封信時，我已經不在人世。我不知道我會在什麼地方、用什麼方式離開，但我確信這是必然的結局，而且結局很快就會到來。請先讀藍彥寫給你的文件，之後如果你想知道更多詳情，就再讀我的自白吧！

你鬱悶的友人

亨利．傑寇

P. 66

「還有第三個信封吧？」亞特森問道。

「先生，在這裡！」卜爾一邊說道，一邊把信拿給他。

第三個是大信封，而且被仔仔細細封好。亞特森先生把信塞進口袋裡，然後對卜爾說：「不要透露這份文件的事，不管你家主人是逃走了或是死亡，我們至少可以讓他留下好名聲。現在已經十點了，我要回家私下讀這些文件，我會在十二點以前趕回來，到時候我們再報警。」

兩人於是走出辦公室，並且把門鎖上。僕人們都聚攏在大廳的火爐旁，亞特森帶著愁容地離開，慢慢走回到自己的辦公室讀那兩份文件，文件會為讓他明白到底發生了什麼事。

信件

- 你想，那兩封是什麼樣的信件？
- 你寫過信件嗎？收過別人寫給你的信嗎？
- 寫一封信給朋友，聊聊你今天的心情。

藍彥博士的講述

P. 67

一月九日那天，也就是四天之前，我接到一封由老友亨利．傑寇所寄來的掛號信。我甚感意外，因為我們一向很少通信，更何況在前一天才剛見過面，一起用過餐，也沒見他提起任何信件的事。我無從揣測他為什麼會寫信來，而且還是用掛號信寄來的。信中所寫的內容，讓我更加不解。信裡頭寫道：

P. 68

親愛的藍彥：

你是我交往最久且感情最好的朋友之一，雖然我們在科學方面的見解不同，但我們仍然友誼常在，我也永遠願意為你赴湯蹈火，而現在，我需要你的幫助。我的性命仰賴在你手中，如果你不能出手相助，我恐怕活不過今晚。

請取消你所有的約會和計畫，然後帶著這封信，叫輛馬車，直接來到我的住處。卜爾已經奉命恭候大駕，然後撬開我的辦公室，你獨自一人走進去，打開標有「E」字樣的櫃子，然後拉開從上面算起的第四個抽屜，把裡面所有東西原封不動地取出，這樣才會知道是否開對了抽屜。現在，我就告訴你裡面有哪些東西，裡頭有一些粉末、一個小玻璃瓶和一本書。請把這些東西連同抽屜都帶回你在凱文迪希廣場的家裡。

這是我務必請你幫忙的第一件事，接下來要交待的是第二件事。如果你現在就立刻出發幫我第一個忙的話，那麼你在半夜之前應該早就回到家。之後在十二點左右，等到大家都已經就寢後，會有一個男人來到你家門口，他會提到我的名字，你一定要親自讓他進門，不要交待僕人處理。接著，你再把從我辦公室裡帶回去的那個抽屜親手轉交給他。如果你要那個人給你一個解釋的話，你到時候就會明白這一切行動都很重要，不然我可能不是沒命就是發瘋。

拜託，拜託，請務必照我的請求去做，這樣一切就都會雨過天晴；反之，後果就會不堪設想。切記，如果照我說的去做，我的所有問題就都會煙消雲散。請務必照我說的去做，以拯救你的老朋友。

亨利．傑寇　敬上

附註：郵局有可能無法在今天晚上遞送，而使得這封信在明天早上才會送到你手中。如果發生這種情況，那就趁著白天看看什麼時候適合，去做我交待的那些事，而那名男子也會在明天半夜再去你家。不過到時候恐怕已經太晚了，所以如果他沒有在半夜出現的話，那你就可能再也看不到老朋友亨利．傑寇了。」

P. 70

當我看到這封信時，心想傑寇一定是瘋了。但在確認情況之前，我覺得應該照他所說的去做。我越不了解所發生的事，就越無從判斷，也越不能輕忽這麼慎重的要求。於是我叫來一輛馬車，直奔傑寇的住處。

卜爾這時已經在等候，原來他也接到了一封掛號信，指示他找來鎖匠和木匠。鎖匠花了兩個小時的功夫，才在沒有鑰匙的情況下打開門，因為木匠表示，那扇門很結實，無法破門而入。

當我們走進辦公室時，我就立刻跑去標有「E」字樣的櫃子，發現櫃子並沒有上鎖。我取出抽屜，用草繩把抽屜裡的東西打包好，以免打破東西，之後再用一件衣服把整個抽屜包起來，然後帶回凱文迪希廣場的家裡。

回到家後，我查看了抽屜裡面的東西。裡頭有一些像鹽一樣的粉狀物，用紙包住，這顯然是傑寇自己準備的，因為這不是原來的包裝。那只小玻璃瓶裡裝了半瓶像血一樣的紅色液體，味道很嗆鼻，我覺得裡面好像有砒霜和一些具揮發性的乙醚成份。

那本書是一本普通的筆記本，除了一連串的日期外，沒記載多少內容。書中的日期跨了好幾年的時間，我發現日期突然在一年前左右停止了。在一些日期的旁邊，有簡短的註記，而且通常只有一、兩個字，像是「加倍」這個字眼，在幾百個日期中出現了六次。還有，在最初的幾個日期裡，出現了「完全失敗」的字眼。我很好奇，但無法從其中嗅出多少端倪。

P. 72

這些玻璃瓶、藥粉和筆記本，顯然和失敗的實驗有關，頂多是如此。而這些再普通不過的東西，怎麼會對朋友的性

命至關重要？我百思不得其解。

我越想越覺得傑寇瘋了，而且這件事可能有危險性。我打發僕人們去就寢，然後找出一把舊式的左輪槍來自衛，在一旁等待著。

半夜一過，便傳來了輕輕的敲門聲。我打開一條小縫，問道：「你是從傑寇博士那裡來的嗎？」

對方是個矮個子，看起來很緊張，回答了一聲「是」，於是我請他進門。

當他一進門，就越過肩頭往後張望，看到黑暗街道的一頭遠遠站著一名警察，於是慌忙地加緊腳步走進屋子裡。

我帶他來到辦公室，我的手始終按著左輪槍。屋內有明亮的燈光，讓我得以把這個人看得清楚。可以確定的是，這是我第一次見到這個人。他個頭矮小，神情驚慌，一付病容，看起來很不安。和他共處一室，讓我覺得很不舒服。

他那種穿著很能讓我發噱。衣服的

質料很好，但尺寸太大，他要捲起褲腳才不會拖在地上，領子鬆垮垮地垂落到雙肩以下，大衣的腰線蓋到了屁股的地方。要是換成其他任何時候，我一定會覺得滑稽，但此刻我一點都笑不出來。我納悶這個讓人討厭的奇怪傢伙究竟是打哪兒來的，他到底想做什麼。

P. 73

這些念頭在我腦海中停留片刻。這位訪客看起來很激動。「你拿到東西了嗎？你拿到東西了沒？」他緊緊抓住我的臂膀，不斷喊道。

我一把推開他的手，可是一碰到他的手，就感覺我全身的血液變冷。

「先生，進來吧，你大概忘了，我還沒那個榮幸認識你，請坐下吧。」我話一說完，就帶頭在我最喜歡的那張椅子上坐下來。

他回答道：「藍彥博士，請原諒我的失禮，你說的沒錯，我太急了，忘記了應有的禮貌。我之所以來訪，是應您同事亨利．傑寇博士的要求，來這裡處理重要的事情。我知道您已經……您已經……」他拼命想保持鎮定，但力有未逮，「我知道……有個抽屜……」

此時此刻，我不禁覺得他有些可憐，「先生，東西在那裡，就在地板上。」我邊說邊用手指向放在書桌後面、被衣服包裹著的抽屜。

他跳起身子，跑向抽屜，然後停下腳步，用手捂住胸口，我聽到了他牙齒打顫的聲音。他的臉色看起來很恐怖，我真怕他斷氣。而當他看到抽屜和裡面的東西時，竟高興得放聲大叫起來。

一時之間，他整個冷靜下來。「你有量杯嗎？」他問道。

P. 74

我從座位上起身，拿了量杯給他，他笑著道謝，然後量出一些紅色的液體倒了進去，接著加入一些粉末。當那些好像鹽一樣的東西倒進去時，液體的顏色開始改變，起初還是紅色，然後變得更加明亮，接著又開始起泡。接著泡沫突然停止了，顏色轉成了深紫色，接下來慢慢褪成淺綠色。

男子從頭到尾一直緊盯著所有的變化，最後把玻璃杯放到桌上，然後扭過頭來對我說：「先生，你是要我默默帶著量杯離開府上，還是要我做一番解釋，來滿足你那種貪婪而無法自拔的好奇心？在回答之前務必要想清楚，因為之後如果後悔也沒有用。你是想要純粹幫朋友的忙，然後完好如初地全身而退，還是想進入一個可怕的新知領域，看看一些雙眼永遠都不敢置信的事？」

我嘴裡冷靜地說道：「先生，別打啞謎了，我並不信任你，這你應該不會感到太訝異。但事情都走到這般田地了，所以我想看到結果。」

「很好，藍彥，記住你身為博士，有守口如瓶的義務。你即將看到的，是我們兩人之間的祕密，只有你和我知道。你以前不相信我的一些科學觀點，現在就請看仔細啦！」

他話一說罷，便把玻璃杯舉到唇邊，一飲而盡。緊接著他大叫一聲，之後一個轉身，搖搖欲墜。他緊緊抓住桌子不放，始終瞪大眼睛，大口大口地喘著氣。

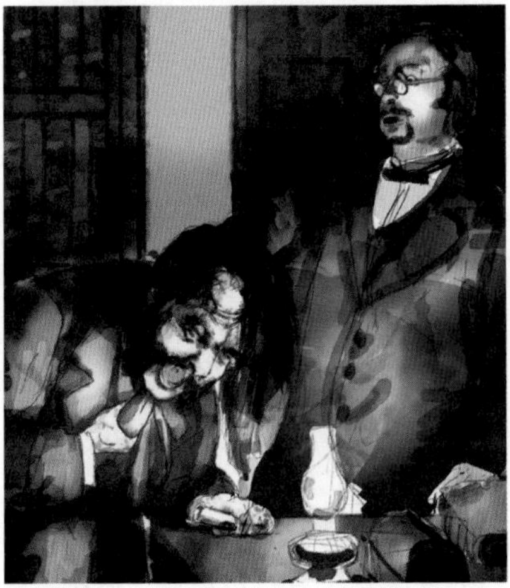

P. 76

就在我觀察著他時，我看到他的外表有了改變。他的身體似乎變大，臉色突然變黑，五官也開始急遽地變化。

「噢，老天！」我尖叫起來。站在我面前的這個男人，他面色蒼白、身體顫抖、呈現半昏迷狀態、不斷伸出雙手摸索，彷彿剛從鬼門關回來，這個人不正是亨利・傑寇嗎？

在接下來的一個小時裡，他跟我說了他的事，我聽得很震驚，不敢置信。我到現在還不知道自己是否相信了這件事，而且沒辦法靜下心把這件事寫下來。我的確看到了我所看見的，也聽到了我所聽見的，但是我卻不知道能否相信自己的眼睛或耳朵。我就是毫無頭緒。

即使到了現在，我還是無法安然入眠，我始終充滿了恐怖和畏懼。我想自己來日無多了，我會在疑惑和恐懼中死去。亞特森，我只告訴你一件事，如果你能相信，就夠了：根據傑寇親口招認，那天半夜來我家的男人，就是由於殺害丹佛・克魯爵士而在英國臭名遠播的愛德華・海德。

哈提斯・藍彥

傑寇與海德

- 傑寇博士和海德先生這兩個角色，是雙重人格者的典型性格。像這樣的角色還有：
  ＊無敵浩克
  ＊雙面人（蝙蝠俠系列）
  ＊克拉克・肯特／超人
- 兩人一組討論這些角色，他們和傑寇／海德的角色有何異同之處？

亨利傑寇的完整自白

P. 77

我出生在一個富裕的家庭。我體格很好，生性勤勉，渴望得到秉性善良之輩的敬重，有一片大好前程。我最大的缺點是太渴望享樂，就像眼前的許許多多人那樣，但我發現，要想一邊享樂、一邊維持我極為重視的尊嚴和良好的聲譽，是一件困難的事。因此，我就把這種嗜好隱藏在不苟言笑和高尚體面的特質之下。

隨著時間的流逝，我「黑暗面」所嗜好的樂趣，變得愈來愈不堪，讓我羞愧不已，並且對我的「光明面」造成很大的困擾和擔憂。

在邁入成年後，我嚴肅地思考自己

的人生和所達到的社會地位。我知道，我生命中值得別人尊敬和追求逸樂的這兩種特質壁壘分明。我的這兩種特質在本質上就相差十萬八千里，彼此水火不容。許多人並不擔心這樣的歧異，甚至會很高興把他們所做的每件事和所有人分享，但我不是這種人，我會覺得很羞愧。我對未來的理想和抱負是那麼地崇高，我想把和人生目標相違的人格特質隱藏起來。

P.78

因此，我的抱負所帶來的問題，遠超過我的任何缺點。絕大多數人的善惡是互相消長的，可是在我身上，這兩者卻是涇渭分明，我忠於兩者，但各行其是。

這種情況讓我思索了很多人類善與惡的雙重特質。我工作認真，一如玩樂時那樣全力以赴，在我的科學研究中，我開始認為人並非只有一個特質或是人格，而是有雙重人格，不過，也就是這樣的發現才毀了我這一生。我之所以會說人類具有兩種人格，是因為這是我知識範圍的極限了。也許在未來，科學家會有更多的發現，發現人類不是只有兩種人格特質而已，一個人可能會有各種差距極大的人格特質。

在我個人身上，可以清楚地看到兩種截然不同的特質。我開始想，這兩種特質是否可以分離成兩個各自獨立的個體——分離成兩個不同身體、不同長相的人。我開始幻想著這樣的可能性，在我的科學實驗顯示這種可能性之前，我就天馬行空地幻想了。如果這兩種特質可以完全分離開來，那麼我的「光明面」就不必為雙重性格之間的巨大差異感到如此憂心，這樣我會活得輕鬆一些。我的「黑暗面」可以為所欲為，不會困擾我的「光明面」。問題是，要如何讓這兩種人格特質分離？

人格特質

- 想想你自己的人格特質，你有哪些優點？又有哪些缺點？
- 有什麼優缺點是你想改變的嗎？

P.79

我不會扯太多科學根據，但我在實驗中開始見識到，有一些藥物能夠改變人類的肉體和心靈，並且活生生的展現出來。我了解到，我們的身體不僅僅是血肉之軀而已，我更清楚地看到，心靈在我們每個人身上所可能帶來的無窮力量。它不是由物質所組成，無法加以捕捉和檢視。

你之後會知道，我的實驗尚未完成，不過可以說我已經有辦法製造出一種藥物，可以讓我「黑暗面」的第二組身體

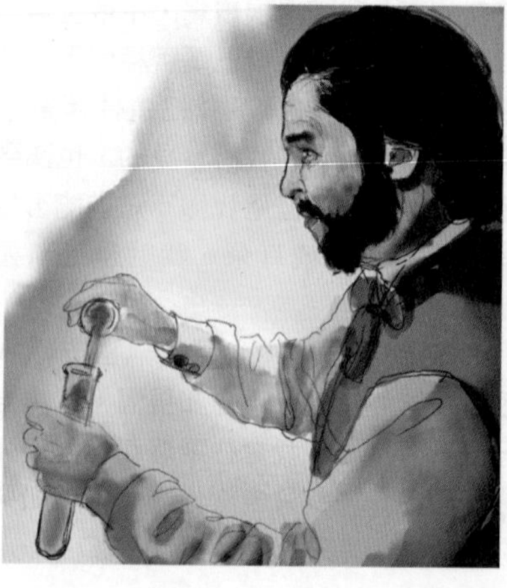

和心靈，取代「正常的」亨利·傑寇的身體和心靈。

我在將理論付諸實驗之前，也曾猶豫過。我很清楚我在冒著死亡的風險，我很可能會完成失去我這個亨利·傑寇的身心，永遠再也變不回來。然而，科學發現的誘惑如此強烈，所以我克服了恐懼。我買了很多特殊的鹽，我從實驗中得知，這是最後所需的成份。

P. 81

有一天晚上，我在實驗室裡把那些成份混在一起，看著它們沸騰，冒出濃煙。當一切就緒，我就喝了藥水。

我第一次服用那種藥物時，真是痛徹心肺。我的骨頭很痛，而且覺得噁心，精神上受到極大的恐懼。不過這種痛苦的感覺很快就過去，我有大病初癒般的感覺。我有一種全新的感受，那是一種愉悅、年輕、快活的感覺。我感到一種自由，也知道自己變得更加邪惡壞心，而這樣的邪念竟然讓我喜不自勝。我也看到自己的個頭變矮小了，由於當時辦公室裡沒有鏡子，所以我就走出實驗室，來到臥房。在鏡子裡，我第一次看到了愛德華·海德的模樣。

過去我的人生幾乎都是為了傑寇博士而活，現在，我把自己備受壓抑的「黑暗面」都轉移到海德這個新的個體上，這可能就是愛德華·海德會比較瘦小年輕的原因吧，因為他的人格在過去受到壓抑，未能獲得良好的發展。他相貌醜陋，也是想當然耳的事，我欣然接受他，因為他忠實地展現了我的「黑暗面」。同樣地，你可以說，傑寇博士那張親切的臉，呈現的大多是他的「光明面」。我注意到，一旦我化身為海德，大家都不想靠近我。我相信所有人都是善惡相雜，唯獨海德是純惡之人。

我沒有花太多時間在鏡中攬視身為愛德華·海德的我，我得繼續進行第二部分的實驗，那就是看我能否再變回傑寇博士，還是我已經永遠變不回來了。

P. 82

如果我變不回來了，那我就得在天亮之前離開，那裡也將不再是我的家。於是我又重複了實驗一遍，把藥水準備好，一飲而盡。在飽受和前次一樣的痛苦過程後，我又變回了亨利·傑寇的樣子。

那天晚上，我來到攸關生死的十字路口。藥水本身無善惡可言，那不過是藥物罷了，在當時，我還有機會好好利用它。我現在有了兩種人格和兩種外貌，一個是純惡之人，另一個依舊是亨利·傑寇，傑寇善惡交雜，我一直想改造他。

在過去，亨利·傑寇仍會渴望著尋歡作樂，但他的社會地位不容許他縱情於不體面的享樂之中。因此對我來說，與其當一個德高望重的傑寇博士，倒不如做愛德華．海德，享受低級的趣味。

那種藥水不難製作，而且就像變裝一樣，不消片刻就可以變成海德。我以變成海德為樂，不過這兩個形體都是我，而且兩者都讓我感到很自在。我開始安排我的生活，以便善加利用這種情況。

變身

‧為什麼傑寇會選擇變成海德？在下列答案中挑出最正確的打勾。

□因為他想繼續進行他的科學研究

□因為他不想再為人所敬重

□因為他想利用海德的身分來尋樂

P. 83

我在蘇活區買了房子，好讓海德有一處棲身之所，並且雇用了一位話不多、不怎麼體面的婦人當管家，以免她東問西的。我跟僕人們說，海德可以自由使用我的房子和一切財產，我會三不五時變身成海德，來到傑寇的住所，好讓僕人們習慣於這樣的安排。我甚至寫了一份有利於海德的遺囑。亞特森，就是那份你並不喜歡的遺囑。但我非得這麼做不可，這樣萬一傑寇有個三長兩短，我才可以用邪惡的海德先生身分，繼續活下去。

用這種方式，我可以過著兩種截然不同的人生，一方面過著受人尊敬的生活，另一方面也可以尋歡作樂。當我知道不管發生什麼事，我都可以保住我的金錢和財產，那我就可以安全無虞地分別過著這兩種生活。

我覺得很有安全感，當我化身為愛德華．海德時，我可以胡作非為、為所欲為，而我也可以隨時變回備受尊崇的亨利．傑寇。天下之大竟沒有一人可以逮到我，我不用負一丁點的責任。

我喜歡做的事並不光彩，在變身成海德先生之後，這些嗜好變得更加恐怖。有時候亨利．傑寇也被會海德的惡行給嚇到，但他覺得自己毋須為此負責，那是海德，又不是他。傑寇仍舊擁有良好的人格特質，甚至如果情況許可，他還會替海德的惡行收拾爛攤子，但儘管如此，他仍然覺得自己不用負責任。

P. 84

當我開始走上這條路時，我不清楚最後會走向什麼樣的結局。雖然我不知道可能的後果，但我對事情的演變有了一些警戒。我可以給你舉個例子，只是這件事情後來並沒有導致最壞的結果。

我有一次在馬路上，不小心撞倒了一個小女孩，結果我大發脾氣，踢了小女孩，有一個路人看了憤憤不平。隔天我認出來那個路人就是你的表弟，小女孩的家人和醫生隨後也趕來，我一時覺得自己小命難保。他們全部的人都義憤填膺，婦女們語出威脅，所以我想最好還是花錢消災，讓他們閉嘴滾開。

我當時是愛德華．海德，只好帶他們到傑寇的實驗室門口，付給他們一張由亨利．傑寇的名字所開立的支票，這一定會讓他們覺得很奇怪。在這件事發生之後，我決定用愛德華．海德的名字，在銀行另外開個戶頭，以杜絕後患。

接著到了丹佛．克魯爵士遇害之前的兩個月左右，有一天我因為遊蕩得太晚，很晚才回到傑寇的家，變身回傑寇後便倒頭就睡。隔天，我醒來時已經日上三竿，我慢慢開始覺得有些不對勁，但因為我當時還很睏，所以不太引以為意，然後繼續倒頭大睡。

沒多久，我又醒了過來，無意中看到自己擱在床單上的那隻手，我嚇了一大跳，因為那不是亨利．傑寇那隻粗壯結實的手，而是愛德華．海德那隻瘦削黝黑又毛茸茸的手。

P. 86

我嚇得從床上跳起來，奔到鏡子前，我看到鏡子裡瞪著我看的是海德，我嚇得全身發冷。昨晚上床的明明是亨利．傑寇，醒來後怎麼會變成愛德華．海德？這是怎麼回事？要如何讓此事不再發生？

我很害怕。我得去實驗室，但是在早上這種時候，我要如何避開僕人穿過房子？我的藥都放在辦公室裡，要走到那裡還要一段路，我得走下兩段樓梯，再沿著走廊穿過庭院，走到實驗室的最裡面。我可以用東西把臉遮住，但我的身材該如何掩飾？

後來我突然想到，這根本就不是什麼問題嘛！僕人們早就認識海德了，儘管他們還不曾在大白天的這種時候看過他。於是我換上傑寇的衣服，盡量把自己打理得像樣些，然後穿過屋子。僕人們在這時候看到我這一身裝扮，不由得兩眼發直。然而十分鐘之後，傑寇博士便恢復了原本的容貌，並且和往常一樣，坐在那兒享用著早點。

你可以想像得到，我胃口不大。這次讓人費解的意外，迫使我以更慎重的態度來思索雙重存在的各種問題和可能性。海德的人格變得愈來愈強烈，我開始意識到可能帶來的危險，如果這種情形持續下去，愛德華．海德的人格早晚會喧賓奪主。

為了停止變身成海德，我早就服用更大量的藥水了。一剛開始比較困難的地方，是如何由傑寇變成海德，但我後來逐漸喪失原來那個較好的自己，慢慢變成較差的第二個自己。

P. 87

如今，我覺得有需要在這兩個身分之間做個抉擇，我該如何做出決定？這兩個身分的唯一共通處，就是他們擁有相同的記憶，其他的就都不一樣子。

真正混合著這兩個面的是傑寇，他分享著海德的冒險行為，而且有時還會樂在其中，儘管他並非事事認同海德。相較之下，海德對傑寇的生活興趣缺缺，而且只有零星的記憶。傑寇很關心海德，就像父親對兒子一樣；但海德對傑寇漠不關心，連兒子對父親的那種關愛都沒有。

變回傑寇，意味著我會失去曾經有過

的快樂；變成海德，則意味著失去傑寇無窮的興趣和抱負，包括失去他所有的朋友。這個抉擇看似簡單，變成海德後會失去的東西比較多，但事情並非這簡單，因為儘管變回傑寇會因為沒有了人生的樂趣而悵然若失，但對海德來說，是不會有任何失落感的。

抉擇
- 為什麼要選擇變成海德？又為什麼要選擇變回傑寇？
- 你曾經面臨過困難的抉擇嗎？那是什麼事？你當時是如何下決定的？

P. 88

雖然這和之前所遇到的狀況不盡相同，可是我還是像許多其他的人一樣，決定選擇保留我比較好的那一面，變回傑寇博士。於是在整整兩個月的時間裡，我都是傑寇博士，只當傑寇博士，但我缺乏足夠的毅力來守住誓言。我一直把海德的衣服給留在辦公室裡，海德的住處也沒打算賣掉，或許由這些事實即可以看出來，我並沒有準備永遠放棄海德這個身分。但在這整整兩個月的時間裡，我謹守著當初所做的決定，我單純地過著生活，努力工作。

不過，隨著時光的流逝，海德在我心所留下的可怕回憶開始淡去，我又開始渴望他所帶來的那種快感。最後，我在一個意志薄弱的時刻，又做了藥水吞下去。但我並沒有做好準備來面對完全缺乏道德、隨時要做壞事的海德。這個惡魔被我禁錮了兩個月，當他再次現身時，他變得比之前更加猖狂惡毒了。

當藥水一生效，我立刻陷入瘋狂，隨即在馬路上攻擊一個朝著我、彬彬有禮走過來的男人。這個受害者在毫無預警、還來不及反應的情況下被打倒在地上。我冷血又無情，享受著每一次的出手，我不停地痛毆受害者，直到他倒地身亡，滿腔怒火的我，一直到手軟了才住手。接著我才突然意識到自己的人生危在旦夕，於是急忙逃離暴行的現場，回到位於蘇活區的海德住處，把文件銷毀掉。接下來我直奔傑寇的家，一路上反覆思索我剛才的行為，想著日後還來進行類似的攻擊。

P. 91

當我再度變回傑寇後，海德的喜悅變成了悔恨和痛苦的眼淚。我看著自己的人生在眼前消逝，我畢生的努力和成就，就在那個可怕的夜晚劃下句點。不管我要不要，我知道我都不能再變成海德了，我只能用傑寇的角色活下去，這是我的比較好的那一面，這樣的想法讓我雀躍不已！我把海德進出的門給鎖上，然後把鑰匙弄壞，這樣他就永遠再也進不來。

第二天，我聽到了凶殺案的新聞，聽說被害人是一個人緣極佳的人，而且大家都知道凶手就是一個叫海德的人。這個理由足夠讓我永遠都不要再變成海德了，而且我也明白這種殺害行為愚不可及。如果再變成海德，那等於我就死路一條了。

因此從那時候開始，我決定要過一個行善的人生。我喜歡這種清清白白的生活，但我的雙重人格有時候仍會困擾著我。我不想再過著像海德那樣的生活了，光是想到這一點就令我害怕。然而，我仍不時地感覺到，我潛藏在表面下的黑暗面在咆哮著。

一月裡，這天天氣晴朗，我坐在攝政公園裡曬太陽。這時，我體內的獸性正夢想著過去的事，而我靈性的那一面則做出允諾，表明我會立刻拋掉這些念頭。就在這個時候，我突然一陣可怕的噁心感，接著就開始感到我的想法和情緒出現變化。我低頭俯視，看到身上的衣服披在小了一號的身體上，而我擱在膝蓋上的手也變得粗糙、毛茸茸的。我又變身為愛德華．海德了，這是全倫敦都在通緝的殺人犯。

P. 92

我只有靠著藥水才能夠變回亨利．傑寇，但是我要如何順利地拿到藥水而不會被逮捕？我專注地思索著問題，其實早在變身為愛德華．海德之前，我就稍稍想過了。傑寇後來大概就放棄了，但是海德沒有，他機靈得很，一定要找出辦法。

我的藥就放在傑寇辦公室裡的櫃子抽屜中，我要怎麼拿到藥？我絞盡腦汁想要解決這個問題。後門已經被我上鎖，而且我把鑰匙弄壞了，所以我無法從後門進入實驗室。如果要從前門進去，僕人一定會看到我，然後把我抓住，移送給警察。我知道我需要找人幫我去拿藥，念頭一轉我就想到了藍彥博士，他可以進到我的房子裡，幫我把藥從辦公室裡拿出來。

我要怎麼請他幫我做這件事？我知道他不喜歡海德，我要怎麼要求一位體面的紳士闖入朋友的辦公室——換句話說，是像個樑上君子一樣地闖入？而且就算他願意幫忙，到時候我又要如何才能到他家和他碰頭？我要怎樣做才能順利走進他家，而不會被逮捕？

後來我想到，我還可以用傑寇博士的身分來寫信，可以用傑寇的筆跡寫封短箋給藍彥，他會認出朋友的筆跡，知道信是傑寇寫的。有了這個想法之後，接下來的事就很容易計畫了。

我盡量把自己穿得體面，臉上能遮掩的就盡量遮掩，然後到街上攔了一輛

馬車，要車伕載我去我所知道的一家旅館。車伕看到我怪模怪樣的服裝，忍俊不禁，不過看到我臉色一拉下，他立刻收起笑臉。算他走運，知道應該馬上停下來！他要是繼續笑下去，我會讓他吃不完兜著走。當時我還真想傷害他。

P. 94

到了旅館之後，工作人員帶我到一個僻靜的客房，他們看到我滿臉怒容，都離得我遠遠的，除了照我的吩咐送來紙筆之外。我變身成海德之後，脾氣非常暴躁，而且想傷害別人，甚至是殺人。這種極端的情緒對我來說是一種全新的體驗。

海德努力按捺住滿腔的怒火，寫了兩封信，一封給藍彥，另一封給卜爾，然後叫人用掛號信寄出去。

那一整天，海德（恐怕已經不能說是「我」了）焦躁不安地在旅館那間僻靜的客房裡等待著，無論是他的言行舉止還是那付尊容，都嚇得工作人員退避三舍。當夜色完全籠罩大地後，他叫了輛馬車，在市區的大街小巷裡繞來繞去。他胸中滿是恐懼和怨恨，當他覺得車伕已開始起疑時，便立刻下車，混進夜晚的行人之間。

他穿著不合身的衣服，樣子怪異又嚇人，只見他步伐極快，自言自語著，心中盤算著到底還要熬多久才能等到半夜。路上有一個女孩想要和他攀談，我想她大概是在向他兜售火柴吧。他打了一下她的耳光，嚇得她立刻落荒而逃。

當我在藍彥家裡恢復本尊時，這位博士的驚懼表情讓我渾身不舒服，不過和我變身為海德後所產生的驚懼反應，他那個樣子根本不算什麼。我對警察不再感到害怕，我害怕的是海德始終如影隨形地跟著我。

在藍彥家裡變身回來之後，我以傑寇博士的身分回到家裡。我不太清楚自己在做什麼，一切恍如夢境，但我還是很慶幸自己得以脫逃，回到家之後，我再度感到安全了。我爬上床，很快就沉沉睡去，一覺到天亮。

P. 96

我早上醒來時，身體還很虛弱，但我精神很好。前一天的恐怖情節雖然還沒忘記，但我總算回到家裡了，我的藥就近在咫尺。但是在用過早餐後，當我行經庭院時，突然開始感覺到我又在面臨恐怖的變化了。我設法走到實驗室拿藥，這次我得服下兩倍的藥量，才能變回傑寇。從那一天起，只有服下大量藥物，才能辛苦地變回傑寇，遠離海德的騷擾。

我要是睡著了，那麼我醒來後都會變成海德。因此我盡可能地少睡，而這影響了我的健康，我愈來愈虛弱，而且被恐懼所吞噬。隨著傑寇的日漸孱弱，海德就變得愈來愈強壯，如今傑寇和海德彼此痛恨著，痛恨的程度不相上下。

沒有人遭受過我的這種痛苦，要是沒有走向這場可怕的結局，這種懲罰可能還會再持續許多年。現在，我已經與自己真實的性格徹底分離了，無法再變回在這城市中備受尊崇的傑寇博士。我使用在藥水中的粉末愈來愈少，我就叫人去買更多藥粉回來。我要卜爾跑遍市區內我所知道的每一家藥房，但就是買不到同樣品質的藥粉。起初，我以為找不到像我原來藥粉那麼純的粉末，後來我才了解到，我原來的那批藥粉可能也不夠純，而且正是因為藥粉不純，才有這麼好的藥效。

P. 97

一個星期轉眼已過，我終於即將寫完這封信，同時也用完了最後的一批藥粉。這是亨利・傑寇最後一次可以運用他自己的想法去思考，也是他最後一次可以看到自己的臉。如果在寫這封信時變身為海德的話，我敢說他一定會把信撕毀，因此我要趕快把信寫完，然後放在一個他看不到的地方。

我知道再過半個小時，我就會變身為愛德華・海德，然後在這裡不住地顫抖和哭泣。他到最後會怎麼離開這人世？他會在牢獄裡死去，還是自我了斷？我不知道答案，而且也不在乎。此刻發生在我身上的，是真正的死亡，緊跟在後的，就是海德的喪鐘響起，那並不是我。就此擱筆了，鬱鬱寡歡的亨利・傑寇，我將把他的生命帶到終點。

ANSWER KEY

Before Reading

Page 8

1 (Possible answer)

a) One man is watching another man open a door.

b) A man is bent over. He seems to be choking. Another man is watching.

Page 9

5 a) T b) T c) T d) F e) F f) F

6

c) I think he is Hyde because his face looks colder and more evil than the other two.

Page 10

8

a) 1 b) 4 c) 9 d) 7 e) 6 f) 10
g) 5 h) 8 i) 2 j) 3

9

a) 1 b) 2 c) 4 d) 3

11

a) 6 b) 1 c) 2 d) 5
e) 8 f) 7 g) 3 h) 4

12

a) walking-stick
b) measuring glass
c) powder
d) ashes
e) axe
f) chimney
g) chain
h) doorknocker

Page 19

- It means do not provoke a potentially danger situation that is at the moment calm.

Page 27

- He knows that Dr Jekyll has not described him, because he is Dr Jekyll.

Page 82

- Because he wants to use Hyde for his pleasure-seeking activities.

Page 87

- He would choose to stay as Hyde in order to keep the pleasures he enjoyed.
- He would choose to stay as Jekyll in order to keep his friends, interests and ambitions.

After Reading

Page 100

6 a) F b) D c) F d) T e) T f) T
g) T h) F i) D j) D

Page 101

8 (Possible answer)

a) Letters from Dr Jekyll and Dr Lanyon explain both men's actions and resolve the mystery of the story. Dr Jekyll's will links Utterson and Jekyll.
b) After the murder of Sir Danvers Carew, Jekyll does not want to live as Hyde any more. He decides to dedicate himself to good deeds and to see his friends again.
c) Lanyon stops all contact with Dr Jekyll after he sees the transformation of Hyde into Jekyll.
d) They expect to find Hyde with Jekyll's dead body.
e) He says that he found it difficult to balance the pleasure-seeking side of his personality with the desire to be respectable.

Page 102

11 (Possible answer)

- Stevenson chooses not to describe him in detail because he is more interested in his psychological side than his physical one.

12 (Possible answer)

- Hyde represents pure evil. People become uncomfortable in his presence because they feel this but don't understand what it is.

13 (Possible answer)

- Examples of Hyde not controlling his anger: when he stamps on the small girl who runs into him at a street corner, when he kills Danvers Carew, and when he hits the match girl.

Page 103

18 (Possible answer)

serious, kind, determined, friendly, loyal, patient

Page 104

20

a) 9 b) 3 c) 8 d) 4 e) 11 f) 7
g) 5 h) 1 i) 6 j) 2 k) 10

Page 105

23 (Possible answer)

From	To	About
Dr Jekyll	Mr Utterson	Changes in Dr Jekyll's will.
Mr Hyde	Dr Jekyll	A letter saying that Hyde will not harm Dr Jekyll.
Mr Utterson	Dr Jekyll	A letter asking why Jekyll won't see him.
Dr Jekyll	Mr Utterson	A letter in reply to Utterson's queries stating that Utterson was Jekyll's friend and he should respect Jekyll's wishes to be left alone.
Dr Jekyll	The chemist	Notes asking for the powder Dr Jekyll used in his experiments.
Dr Jekyll	Mr Utterson	A note saying what to read.
Dr Jekyll	Mr Utterson	Dr Jekyll's final will.
Mr Lanyon	Mr Utterson	An explanation of what happened.
Dr Jekyll	Mr Lanyon	A request for help.
Dr Jekyll	Mr Utterson	An explanation of what happened.

25 (Possible answer)

- We find out that Dr Jekyll and Mr Hyde are the same person when we read Dr Lanyon's narrative.

Test

Page 106

1 (Possible answer)

- Mr Utterson and Mr Enfield met. They are friends and walking companions.
- Mr Utterson and Dr Jekyll met. Utterson is Jekyll's lawyer and friend.
- Mr Utterson and Sir Danvers Carew didn't meet in the story but they were acquaintances.
- Mr Utterson and Poole met. Utterson helps Poole to knock down the door to Jekyll's laboratory.
- Mr Utterson and Mr Guest met. Guest is Utterson's head clerk and he looks at Hyde's letter with Utterson.

- Mr Lanyon and Mr Enfield didn't meet.
- Mr Lanyon and Dr Jekyll met. They are old friends.
- Mr Lanyon and Sir Danvers Carew didn't meet.
- Mr Lanyon and Poole didn't meet.
- Mr Lanyon and Mr Guest didn't meet.

- Hyde's housekeeper and Mr Enfield didn't meet.
- Hyde's housekeeper and Dr Jekyll met. He employed her as Mr Hyde's housekeeper.
- Hyde's housekeeper and Sir Danvers Carew didn't meet.
- Hyde's housekeeper and Poole didn't meet.
- Hyde's housekeeper and Mr Guest didn't meet.

- Inspector Newcomen and Mr Enfield didn't meet.
- Inspector Newcomen and Dr Jekyll didn't meet.
- Inspector Newcomen and Sir Danvers Carew didn't meet. Inspector Newcomen probably saw Carew's dead body.
- Inspector Newcomen and Poole didn't meet.
- Inspector Newcomen and Mr Guest didn't meet.

- Mr Hyde and Mr Enfield met. Enfield intervenes when Hyde stamps on the small girl who runs into him.
- Mr Hyde and Dr Jekyll met. They are two different parts of the same person.
- Mr Hyde and Sir Danvers Carew met.
- Mr Hyde and Poole met. Poole is Dr Jekyll's housekeeper and he sometimes sees Hyde in the house.
- Mr Hyde and Mr Guest didn't meet.

Page 107

3 a) 3 b) 2 c) 2 d) 2

Page 108

4

a) The noise had attracted a small crowd of people who were very angry with the man.

b) The check was signed by a man whose name I cannot tell you.

c) He went across the back garden to the building at the back which Jekyll had made into a laboratory.
d) He was small, and he had a shocking expression on his face, which looked both ill and restless.
e) I think your employer could have a very painful illness which also affects his appearance.
f) I went wild and attacked a man who had approached me politely in the street.

Page 109

5

a) Mr Hyde
b) Dr Jekyll
c) Poole
d) Mr Hyde
e) Dr Jekyll
f) Sir Danvers Carew

The Strange Case of Doctor Jekyll and Mr Hyde 化身博士

原 著　Robert Louis Stevenson
改 寫　Les Kirkham, Sandra Oddy and Maria Cleary
譯 者　李璞良
校 對　陳慧莉
封面設計 蔡怡柔
編 輯　黃鈺云
製程管理 洪巧玲
發行人 黃朝萍
出版者 寂天文化事業股份有限公司
電 話　02-2365-9739
傳 真　02-2365-9835
網 址　www.icosmos.com.tw
讀者服務 onlineservice@icosmos.com.tw
出版日期 2023年8月 初版二刷（寂天雲隨身聽APP版）

郵撥帳號 _ 1998620-0 寂天文化事業股份有限公司
訂書金額未滿1000元，請外加運費100元。
〔若有破損，請寄回更換，謝謝。〕

國家圖書館出版品預行編目資料

化身博士 (寂天雲隨身聽 APP 版) / Les Kirkham, Sandra Oddy and Maria Cleary 著 ; 李璞良 譯 . 一
初版 . 一 [臺北市] : 寂天文化， 2023.08
面； 公分 . 中英對照
ISBN 978-626-300-201-2 (25K 平裝)
1.CST: 英語 2.CST: 讀本

805.18　　112010902

Helbling Fiction 寂天現代文學讀本

1 The Kingdom of the Snow Leopard 雪豹王國

2 The Boy Who Could Fly 飛翔吧，男孩

3 Operation Osprey 魚鷹與男孩

4 Red Water 少年駭客的綠色事件簿

5 Danger in the Sun 憂鬱少年的藍色希臘

6 The Coconut Seller 里約小情歌

7 The Green Room 男孩女孩的夏日劇場學園

8 Mystery at the Mill 英倫女孩站出來

9 The Albatross 信天翁號的獵鷹